BIONICLE®
ADVENTURES

Volume 1

BIONICLE®
ADVENTURES

Volume 1

by Greg Farshtey

SCHOLASTIC INC.
New York Toronto London Auckland Sydney
Mexico City New Delhi Hong Kong Buenos Aires

BIONICLE Adventures #1: Mystery of Metru Nui,
ISBN 0-439-60731-0, Copyright © 2003 The LEGO Group.
BIONICLE Adventures #2: Trial by Fire,
ISBN 0-439-60732-9, Copyright © 2003 The LEGO Group.
BIONICLE Adventures #3: The Darkness Below,
ISBN 0-439-60733-7, Copyright © 2004 The LEGO Group.

12 11 10 9 8 7 6 5 4 3 2 1 6 7 8 9/0 1

Printed in the U.S.A. 23

This edition created exclusively for Barnes & Noble, Inc.

2006 Barnes & Noble Books

ISBN 0-7607-9603-3

First compilation printing, January 2006

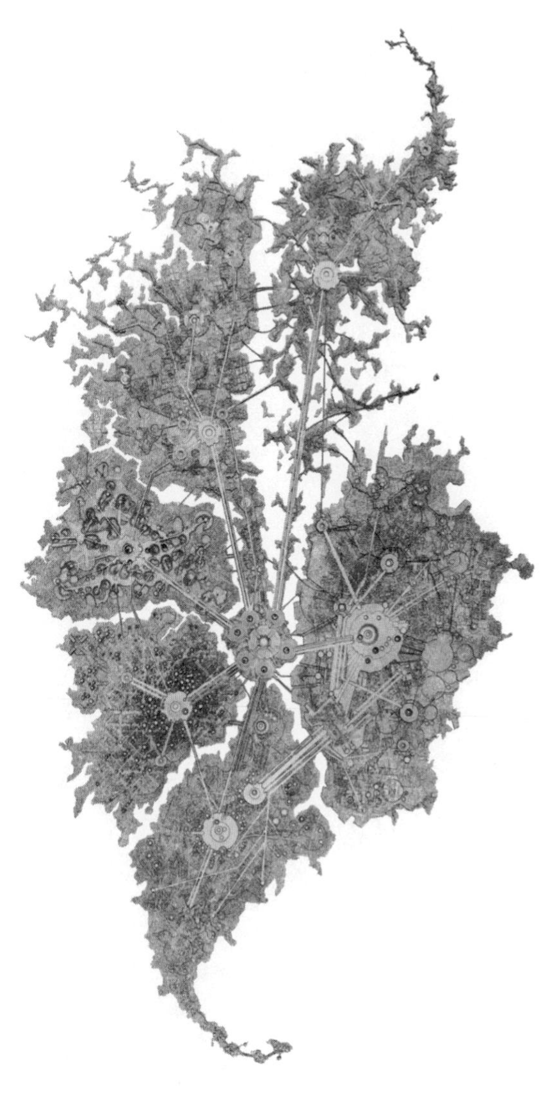

The City of Metru Nui

Contents

BIONICLE®

Mystery of Metru Nui

For Evan, who shows the world every day what being a hero really means, from his best pal.

— GF

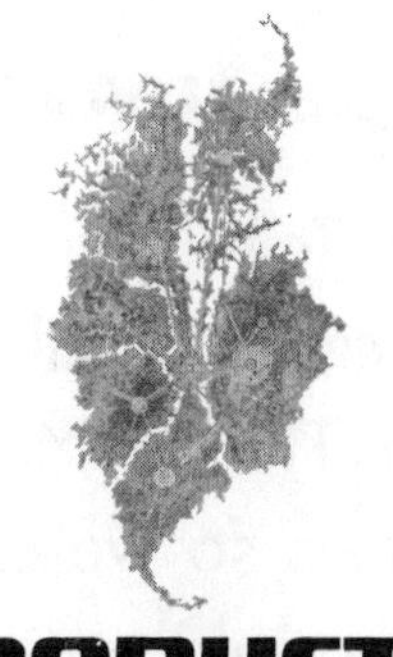

INTRODUCTION

Turaga Vakama, elder of the Mata Nui village of fire, stood on a high cliff overlooking the beach. Far below, Matoran from all over the island were hard at work constructing boats for the long journey back home.

Vakama shook his head. Home. It had been so long since any of them had seen it, and the Matoran did not even remember living anywhere but Mata Nui. Only the six village elders recalled when and why they first came to the island, and for thousands of years, they had locked that secret away inside themselves.

The Turaga turned at the sound of another's approach. It was Tahu Nuva, Toa of Fire and leader of the heroes of Mata Nui. "How go the labors, Turaga?" he asked.

"Quite well, Toa Tahu. We will soon have enough boats to carry us all back to the island city of Metru Nui. The Po-Matoran are at work widening the tunnels so we can carry the boats to the subterranean sea."

Tahu nodded as his mind flashed back to the events of the past months. After the final confrontation with Makuta, master of shadows, the Toa had discovered a new island far beneath the surface of Mata Nui. It sat in the center of a silver sea of protodermis, and they could see few details of it from the shore. But Vakama insisted that this place was Metru Nui, the original home of the Matoran, to which they must return.

Even more startling, the Turaga revealed that Metru Nui had once been home to six other Toa, heroes who existed long before Tahu and the others ever appeared. But Vakama had said nothing about the fate of those early "Toa Metru," or whether they might still be waiting on Metru Nui.

"I have been in council with the other Toa,"

said Tahu. "I have come to ask you to tell us all about this new land, Metru Nui. If we are going to journey there and protect the Matoran from any threats that might lurk in that place, we must know everything."

Vakama turned and walked away from the cliff. "Indeed you must. But I will warn you, Tahu: The tales of Metru Nui are tales of sacrifice, betrayal, great danger, and yes, heroes as well. Their telling may change much of what you think you know about myself, the other Turaga, and the Matoran you have served all this time."

"I — we — are prepared for that, Turaga," replied Tahu. "The Toa have gathered at the Great Temple of Kini-Nui. They wait only for you."

"Then let them wait no longer, Tahu."

The seven Toa — Tahu, Kopaka, Gali, Pohatu, Onua, Lewa, and Takanuva — stood silently around the Amaja Circle. The Turaga had used that sandpit and the stones within it many times to tell tales of the past and future.

The Turaga of Fire placed the stone representing Mata Nui in the center of the circle and began. "In the time before time, long before any Matoran set foot on the island of Mata Nui, there was a city of legends. Hear now the first tale of Metru Nui. . . ."

Kapura walked slowly along the outskirts of the district of Ta-Metru, his eyes scanning the ground. Most of the homes and factories in this part of the metru had been abandoned lately, with the residents moving closer to the heart of the district. It was Kapura's job to make sure nothing of importance had been left behind.

He paused in front of a massive, blackened building that had once housed a forge. Here, construction tools and other equipment had been cast from molten protodermis before being sent on to Po-Metru for finishing. Now, in the interest of safety, that work had been transferred away from the outskirts by order of the city's elder, Turaga Dume. Kapura spotted a staff used in the sport of kolhii on the ground and bent down to pick it up, only to discover the handle was cracked.

He walked on. This was an important task, his fellow workers had told him, and important tasks were best done slowly and carefully.

Had Kapura looked up, he would have seen the skyline of Ta-Metru, "home of the makers." Cone-shaped factories, scorched by ages of use, stood next to the homes of smiths and crafters. These were the Matoran who molded protodermis, the substance of which everything on Metru Nui was made, into thousands of shapes and forms. A molten river of raw protodermis ran through the center of the district, drawn from below the city and fed into the Great Furnace. From there, it traveled to each factory to be turned into masks, tools, and anything else that might be needed.

Dominating the skyline was the Coliseum, home to Turaga Dume and the tallest building in all of Metru Nui. For as long as anyone could remember, the sight of the Coliseum had brought a feeling of safety and security to Matoran. But now . . .

Kapura counted slowly as he walked. Six, seven, eight — at least eight of the workers at his factory had vanished lately. Where they disappeared to, and why, no one knew. But there were plenty of rumors.

The Matoran stopped. Something had moved off to the right. It didn't sound like another Matoran, or even a wild Rahi beast. It was a soft, slithering sound, as if something was dragging itself across the ground. The sound grew louder and seemed to multiply. Kapura felt the urge to run, but his feet would not move.

He forced himself to turn around and look. Four thick, blackened, twisted vines were snaking their way out of cracks in the ground, weaving in the air as if momentarily unsure of what to do. Then they wrapped themselves around the empty factory and began to climb, winding around again and again until they covered the building from top to bottom.

Kapura's eyes widened as the vines started to squeeze. Solid protodermis crumbled before their strength. The building groaned and cracked, collapsing in on itself in a matter of seconds. As if satisfied, the vines pulled away and began to move toward another structure.

It was then that Kapura found his voice. But he could speak only one word, and that in a horrified whisper:

"Morbuzakh."

In another section of the city, a second Matoran was also thinking about the dreaded Morbuzakh plant. The vines had been appearing on the outskirts of the city for some time, wrecking structures and forcing residents to flee. No one knew where they came from or how to stop them. All that was known was that everyone who challenged the Morbuzakh vanished, never to be seen again.

But this particular Matoran wasn't worried about the damage the plant was causing. Instead, all his attention was focused on a tablet decorated with a most interesting carving. The picture showed the combined power of six disks defeating a gigantic Morbuzakh root. Disks — called

Kanoka in the Matoran language — were a common sight in Metru Nui. The spheres were created in every metru and used primarily for sport, as well as for defense against the wild beasts called Rahi. Disks found to be of the right purity and power level were forged into Masks of Power. But the disks in the carving could not simply be any old Kanoka, the Matoran knew. These had to be the six Great Disks of legend.

Under the picture of each Great Disk was inscribed the section of the city where it could be found and the name of a Matoran: Nuhrii, Ahkmou, Vhisola, Tehutti, Ehrye, and Orkahm.

When he was done examining the carving, the Matoran turned to Nidhiki, the strange, four-legged being who had brought it. "What is it I'm supposed to do?"

"I would think it would be obvious," hissed Nidhiki from the shadows. "Get the six Great Disks. I don't care how. Then give them to me and I will take them somewhere . . . safe."

The Matoran frowned. "If they truly exist, these are the six most powerful Kanoka disks in

Metru Nui. They would be beyond price. What do I get out of this?"

"You will be well paid, Matoran," Nidhiki replied, smiling in a particularly nasty way. "Plus you get one more benefit, if you're successful: I won't come looking for you."

"All right, all right. I get the idea. But why is this so important? Even if these Matoran could get their hands on the Great Disks, they wouldn't dare try to stop the Morbuzakh themselves."

"It's not Matoran we're worried about," came the answer. "It's so-called heroes — Toa Metru. Six Toa Metru."

With that, Nidhiki was gone. The Matoran watched him go, thinking, *Six Toa Metru? How is that possible?*

Moments before, they had been Matoran. Six strangers, each from a different metru, brought together by a plea for help from Toa Lhikan, the hero of Metru Nui. Now, in the heart of the Great Temple in Ga-Metru, they had been transformed. Where once six Matoran had stood, there now existed six new Toa Metru.

Whenua, once an archivist in Onu-Metru and now the Toa of Earth, voiced the thoughts of them all. "Since when are Matoran just zapped into Toa?"

Nuju, former seer and now Toa of Ice, answered, "When uncertain times lie ahead."

Vakama, Ta-Metru's most skilled mask maker and the new Toa of Fire, looked down at his new form. It was hard to believe that this new power had been granted to him. He remembered the city's protector, Toa Lhikan, giving him a powerful artifact called a Toa stone and a map to a spot in the Great Temple. Then Lhikan was captured by two strange creatures, one a four-legged foe and the other huge and powerful. Heeding his last wish, Vakama had taken the Toa stone to the temple, only to run into five other Matoran with similar missions.

They placed their stones on top of the shrine dedicated to Toa. Before their eyes, the

Toa stones began to pulsate and then rose into the air. Beams of elemental energy shot from them, bathing the Matoran in light, changing them, granting them power. When it was over, the Matoran had become Toa Metru, destined guardians of Metru Nui.

But are we ready for this? Am I? Vakama asked himself. He didn't have an answer.

The other Toa had begun selecting their tools from a compartment inside the suva shrine. Vakama looked over what remained and chose a powerful Kanoka disk launcher. It was a larger version of what he had used in the past to play the sport of kolhii. The familiarity of it made him feel a little more comfortable in his new body.

Matau, Toa of Air, chuckled. "Nice choice — for playing Matoran games, mask maker."

"Hey, look at this," Onewa, the new Toa Metru of Stone, said. He reached into the tool compartment and emerged with six Kanoka disks. Each was a different color, and each bore the likeness of a Mask of Power. But what drew the attention of the new heroes was that the masks matched the ones they now wore.

"What does it mean?" asked Nokama, Toa Metru of Water.

"Perhaps that we were not chosen at random for this?" Vakama suggested. "Perhaps this is our destiny."

"What did Toa Lhikan say we could expect, Vakama? What are we meant to do now that we are Toa?" asked Whenua. Nokama and Onewa drew in closer, anxious to hear the answer as well.

"He said —" Vakama began.

Then, suddenly, his mind was somewhere else. He could see day being consumed by night, Metru Nui collapsing into ruin, then miraculously restored. Six Kanoka disks flew at him from out of the darkness, forcing him to duck and dodge. They shot past him, then hovered in the air and unleashed their power on the Morbuzakh plant. Before their energies, the plant withered and died. Their task done, the Great Disks merged together to form a single one of immense power, and . . .

Then the vision was gone. But the chill inside Vakama told him it had not just been an idle daydream. "Metru Nui was destroyed. I saw it! Six Great Kanoka Disks were headed right for me, and . . ."

"Thanks for dream-sharing," Matau said, shaking his head.

"No, we must find them. They can defeat the Morbuzakh and free the city from danger. That would prove we are worthy to be Toa Metru!" Vakama continued.

The others looked at him, some doubtful, some evidently willing to believe. They had all heard the tales of the Great Disks before. It was said they contained enormous power, but the only clue to their location was that one was hidden in each metru. If the disks were used by someone with good intent, they could change the world for the better. If their user was evil, Metru Nui and all its inhabitants might be erased forever.

"Then find them we shall," said Nokama. "I saw a carving in the temple that might help us.

Something about finding the Great Disks by seeking the unfamiliar within the familiar. But the rest seemed to be . . . riddles. What do you think, Vakama?"

But the Toa of Fire was not listening. In his mind's eye, he saw six Matoran, each with a Great Disk. He knew their names but could not see their faces. Worse, the shadows behind them were alive with danger. Vakama could see a pair of fierce red eyes hovering in the darkness and a four-legged creature stalking the Matoran. He had seen that figure before, in real life, struggling with Toa Lhikan. Vakama knew how powerful and evil this being was, and the memory made him shudder.

"Nuhrii . . . Orkahm . . . Vhisola . . . Ahkmou . . . Ehrye . . . Tehutti," Vakama muttered. "They can decipher the riddles. They can help us find the Great Disks. But beware of a dark hunter who walks on four legs."

"You have spent too much time at the forge, fire-spitter," answered Onewa. "Your head needs cooling down."

"I trust Vakama," Nokama said. "If he believes those six Matoran can help us find the disks, then we must seek them out. When we have found them, we will meet back here. Good luck to us all."

If my vision is true, thought Vakama, *we will need far, far more than luck.*

The Toa Metru said their farewells and went their separate ways. Only Nokama and Vakama remained behind, staring up at the Great Temple.

"Vakama, do you really think Metru Nui is in danger? Perhaps from something more frightening than the Morbuzakh?"

"I know there is darkness coming," Vakama replied. "Toa Lhikan said we had to stop it. He said we had to save the 'heart of the city.' I don't know how or why, but we have been chosen."

"Then may the Great Beings protect us all," said the Toa of Water.

Toa Nokama turned and began walking farther into Ga-Metru. All was quiet. This was traditionally the most peaceful section of Metru Nui, home to scholars and scientists. Often the only sound that could be heard was the rush of the protodermis falls.

Ga-Matoran passed her on the street, looking up with awe and wonder. Some were old friends, but no one seemed to recognize her. When she did stop someone and say hello, the Matoran shied away from her and scurried off.

Nokama frowned. She had never nursed any dreams of becoming a Toa. She enjoyed her life as a teacher in Ga-Metru, gaining new wisdom each day and passing it on to others. Her happiest moments had been spent in a classroom or showing her students the ancient carvings at the protodermis fountains. Now that she was a "hero," she was starting to realize what a lonely role it could be.

At least my very first task will not be a hard one, she thought. *Vhisola will gladly help me.*

As she walked along the canals past the beautiful temples of Ga-Metru, she remembered when she had first met her friend. Vhisola had been a student in one of Nokama's classes. The Ga-Matoran had been eager to learn, almost too eager. In her enthusiasm, she always seemed to make some mistake or other. Then she would get flustered and make another and another, until her project was a mess.

Eventually, Nokama realized that if she spent extra time with Vhisola, the Matoran did better work. They became friends and still were, even if sometimes it was a stormy friendship. The more time they spent together, the more time Vhisola wanted to spend. If Nokama said she was too busy to practice kolhii or explore the canals that day, Vhisola would sulk.

Their last argument had been a bad one, but Nokama was certain they had patched things up. Certainly Vhisola would not hesitate to help if she knew the fate of the city depended upon it.

Nokama rapped on the door of Vhisola's small home. No one answered. When she rapped again, one of the neighbors emerged and said, "Who are you?"

"I'm —" Nokama began, then hesitated. If she gave her name, she would probably have to give a long explanation of why she was no longer a Matoran. Instead, she replied, "I'm the Toa of Water. Have you seen Vhisola?"

"A Toa? Here?" said the Ga-Matoran excitedly. "I know of Toa Lhikan, of course, but I have never met a Toa up close. Where did you come from? Are you here to stay?"

"Please, just answer my question. Have you seen Vhisola today?"

The Ga-Matoran shook her head. "No, not lately. Is she in some trouble?"

"I hope not," Nokama said. She tried the door, but it was locked. Still, she was now a Toa, and much stronger than before. A little bit of force and the door flew open.

Although they had known each other a long time, Nokama had never been inside Vhisola's home. Now she saw why. Every inch of the walls was covered with carvings of Nokama, records of her achievements, copies of awards she had won. There was nothing in the room to say that Vhisola even lived there.

Once the shock had passed, Nokama began to look around for any sign of where Vhisola might have gone. Her eye was caught by lights flashing on a table. Coming closer, she saw that the lights were part of a map of Ga-Metru. Certain sections lit up, flashed for an instant, then went dark again. With no better idea, Nokama moved her hand from section to section as they lit, hoping to find a pattern.

There was a sound of stone grinding against stone. Then the center of the map opened up and a tablet rose from inside the table. Nokama picked it up and saw it was Vhisola's journal. She almost put it back — then she remembered the real fear in Vakama's face when he spoke of his visions. If Metru Nui was in danger, Nokama could not afford to ignore any possible clue.

She scanned the last few entries and found nothing of note. But the last left her numb with fear. It read: "At first, I couldn't believe it when I heard Nokama was a Toa. Now that she is a hero, she will never have any time for me. I've spent so much time practicing my kolhii and trying to do better schoolwork, all to impress her . . . and now she will just want to spend time with her new Toa friends. Well, I'll show her. Once I get my hands on that Great Disk, I'll be the one people have to look up to. She will be the one they ignore!"

She knows I am a Toa? How . . . ? Oh, Vhisola, Nokama said to herself, *I never meant to ignore you. You don't know the danger you could be in.*

There was no time for worry or regret. There were only two other places Vhisola spent time at, the school and the kolhii practice field. There was no practice scheduled for today, so maybe she was in class. If she wasn't, it might already be too late.

Nokama turned to leave, then stopped. Out the window, she could see the familiar, spiderlike shapes of Vahki moving down the avenue. They enforced the law and kept order in Metru Nui, but even so, the sight of them had always filled Nokama with an unnamed dread. Vhisola's neighbor was talking to the squad leader.

Maybe she sent for them, Nokama thought. *Maybe she doesn't believe I am a Toa — especially since I can hardly believe it myself.*

The Vahki would want to bring her to Turaga Dume for questioning, and there was no time for that. She would have to get away from them.

Outside the house, the Ga-Matoran neighbor was doing her best to make the Vahki understand. "She said she was a Toa. Well, how do I know that's what she is? Maybe it's some trick of the Morbuzakh. Anyway, I know my duty, so I sent for you."

The Vahki nodded and signaled to the others in its squad to surround the house. Once certain that its stun staff was fully charged, it headed for Vhisola's home.

Nokama chose that moment to burst out of the door. Before the Vahki could react, she rushed past him and dove into the protodermis canal. Extending her hydro blades in front of her, she knifed through the liquid. The Vahki wasted no time in pursuing, taking to the sky to follow her course.

No Matoran could hope to outdistance a Vahki, but a Toa was another matter. Her Toa tools gave her an edge in speed, though she knew it would not be enough. She would have to rely on her most powerful advantage — her knowledge of Ga-Metru.

Up ahead, the canal continued toward the Great Temple, but there was a narrow branch to the left that fed protodermis into a central reservoir. Nokama glanced over her shoulder. The Vahki were temporarily out of sight. She whipped around the corner and down the feeder branch, plunging into the reservoir far below.

Nokama dove deep into the cool protodermis, then kicked hard and broke the surface. The reservoir was a huge, circular chamber, lit by lightstones embedded in the ceiling. Every sound echoed and re-echoed in the chamber, from the lapping of the waves to Nokama's breathing. But the one sound she did not hear was Vahki up above.

Satisfied that they had given up, Nokama dove down to the bottom of the tank and swam into another feeder branch. *The other Toa have probably already found their Matoran,* she thought. *How they will laugh when they hear of the difficulty I had!*

Vhisola's classes were held in one of the many ornate domes that dotted Ga-Metru. Her instructor was little help but did suggest that perhaps the Matoran had closeted herself in the lab to finish some overdue work.

It was only a short walk to the lab, but for some reason Nokama felt she had to run. The sight of the door blown off its hinges told her she was already too late.

The inside of the lab looked worse. Furniture was overturned, tablets scattered and smashed as if a windstorm had torn through the place. A lab worker was doing his best to straighten up when Nokama entered.

"What happened here?"

The Matoran jumped. "Don't do that! You startled me! I thought that . . . thing had come back here again."

"I'm sorry," Nokama said, realizing that her new appearance probably was a bit intimidating. "What 'thing' are you talking about?"

"I don't know. Four legs, some kind of claw tool — ripped the place apart. He stole all of Vhisola's research notes, all except one." The Matoran pointed to a shattered tablet on the ground.

Nokama knelt down and began sifting through the fragments, matching the carvings on them together like a puzzle. When she was done, there was an image of a huge Morbuzakh root and six Great Disks bringing it down. Beneath each disk was written the metru it came from and a three-digit code.

Vakama was right! There is a connection between the Great Disks and the Morbuzakh. But why would anyone want to stop us from ending that threat?

Then she caught sight of something else, half hidden by an overturned bench. It was a map of the Le-Metru chute system, stamped with the name Orkahm. *What would this be doing here?* Nokama wondered.

She looked up at the lab worker, who was watching her intently. "The rest of her notes — have you seen them?"

"Hey, I just take care of the lab. I never —"

Nokama rose to her full height. Looking down on the Matoran, she repeated slowly, "Have you seen them?"

The Matoran's gaze dropped to the floor. "All right. She showed them to me once. Said something about a Great Disk making her somebody. Her notes were all about the Morbuzakh, but they didn't make any sense to me. She made copies of everything and said she was taking them home."

"For the sake of Ga-Metru and the whole city, I hope they are still there," said Nokama.

She returned to Vhisola's home through the canals. As she feared, there was still a Vahki patrolling the area. Reasoning with it would be a waste of time. Vahki didn't listen. They were trained to see movement and to react. She needed a distraction.

Well, I am supposed to be the Toa of Water, she said to herself. *Let us see if that is only a name.*

It was the hardest thing Nokama had ever attempted. Extending her twin tools, she strained to draw moisture from the air. At one point, she thought sure she would black out and drift away on the canal. But finally, she could feel one of the most powerful of elements coming under her control.

Two narrow streams of water were all she could manage at first, but they were enough. She targeted a bit of ornamentation on a house down the avenue. The water struck it head-on, knocking it from its perch with a resounding crash. The Vahki paused, turned, and moved off to investigate.

Nokama bolted for the house. Inside, she searched frantically for any possible hiding place. The four-legged creature had obviously not been here, unless he had suddenly grown neater. But where had Vhisola hidden the notes? What would be the one place that would be special to her?

Then her eyes settled on the largest picture of herself. Nokama almost dreaded being proven right, but she was — behind the picture was a safe with three dials. There was no time to try to guess the combination. It had to be one of the codes that had been on the tablet, or her search would end in failure.

At first, she considered using the Ga-Metru code, but that almost seemed too obvious. She tried the Ta-Metru code, the Onu-Metru code, the Po-Metru code, and the others, all to no end. But when she spun the dial to the three digits of the Ga-Metru code, the door swung open. Inside was a pile of tablets, all with Vhisola's distinctive carvings on them. Nokama glanced at each one until she found the crucial piece of information.

It was a carving of the Great Temple with a powerful disk pictured beside it. It had been there all the time!

Vhisola must have gone there to retrieve the Great Disk, thought Nokama. *But if she doesn't know about that four-legged monster . . .*

Nokama turned and raced out of the house. She didn't even worry that the Vahki might pursue her again. *Let it follow me! I could use the help!*

As she sped through the canals heading for the Great Temple, Nokama remembered one of her first conversations with Vhisola. "Everyone has a special talent," she had told the Matoran. "You simply have to discover the one that is yours." Now that she knew Vhisola's plan had been to take the Great Disk for herself and use it for personal gain, she wondered if the Matoran's "special talent" was deception.

She emerged from the canals near the temple but was stopped short by the sight of a crowd of Matoran some distance away. They were craning their necks to look up at one of the tall buildings, pointing and shouting.

Nokama rushed over to them. "What is it? What's happening?"

"It's Vhisola!" one shouted. "On top of that building! She's going to fall!"

The Toa of Water looked up. There was Vhisola, teetering on the edge of a roof. The Matoran wasn't going to be able to maintain her balance for long. Nokama felt helpless. She wasn't a climber, she could never scale the building in time.

She turned and leaped into the canal, extending her hydro blades in front of her. Her momentum carried her forward, skiing across the surface of the canal. Just before reaching a bridge, Nokama dove beneath the surface. She sped through the winding protodermis pipe, down a grade, and back up at incredible velocity. Powered by her fear for Vhisola's life, she flew out of the end of the pipe and soared high into the air, angling her body so she would land on the same roof as the Matoran.

Vhisola saw her coming, rocked a little, and started to fall. Nokama swooped down, caught the Matoran with one arm and the edge of the roof with the other, and hauled them both to safety.

If she expected gratitude, she was disappointed. "You," said Vhisola. "I knew it would be you. Now that you're a Toa Metru, you'll just cast an even longer shadow over me."

"Vhisola, whatever you think, we can deal with it later. I need that Great Disk!"

"Everyone wants my disk," said Vhisola. "Some four-legged thing — not a Rahi, I don't know what it was — chased me through the streets. I had to hide up here to get away from him. I never should have paid attention to that note."

"What note?"

Vhisola produced two small tablets. On the first was a jumble of Matoran numbers, on the second a code key. "Here. Let's see if you can decode it faster than I did."

It took Nokama a few long moments, but finally she was able to read the message. It said: "Beware. The Toa serve the Morbuzakh. They must not find the Great Disks. Meet me at the protodermis falls with your disk and I will keep it safe. Ahkmou."

Nokama suddenly felt very cold. "Come on, Vhisola. We need to have a long talk with some friends of mine."

Ask a Ga-Matoran or a Ko-Matoran, and they would say Ta-Metru was the harshest, least hospitable spot in all of Metru Nui. The searing heat of the forges and the Great Furnace, the heavy smell of molten protodermis, the constant sound of crafters hammering away — to Matoran from the quieter districts, Ta-Metru was a nightmare.

Vakama, Toa of Fire, would have agreed with that opinion right now, if he'd had a moment to think. Instead, he was diving and rolling to avoid white-hot protodermis flowing from a vat high above. An accidental overflow or leak was always bad news, but in this case, it was far worse than that.

Vakama glanced up. Yes, the Morbuzakh vines were still there, trying hard to rip the protodermis vat off its chain and hurl it to the ground. If they succeeded, there might not be much left of this section of Ta-Metru.

The Toa's mind raced. Morbuzakh vines had never been seen this far inside a metru. Protodermis vats on their way to a forge should never stall long enough for anything to grab hold of them. But both had happened, and just when Vakama arrived in search of a missing mask maker.

Ta-Matoran workers were running for cover. But if enough hot protodermis hit the ground, there would be no place to hide. It would burn through anything in its path unless Vakama found a way to stop it.

Right. Sounds easy, thought the new Toa Metru. *Only how do I do it? I can't keep ducking and dodging. The vat is too high up to reach by climbing. Not that the Morbuzakh will let me get close enough anyway. Unless . . .*

Matau had made fun of his choice of a disk launcher for a Toa tool. But right now, Vakama felt like it was the wisest decision he had ever made. He looked at the three-digit code on one of his disks. The first digit identified where it was made, the second its power, the third its power level. This was a level 5 freeze disk. Better still, the disk had been made in Ko-Metru, which meant it carried an extra surprise for the Morbuzakh vines.

Vakama rolled, came up in a crouch, aimed, and let the disk fly. As he expected, the Morbuzakh vines reacted instantly, swiping at the spinning object. But Ko-Metru disks were made to swerve at high speed to avoid any obstacle. The Morbuzakh grasped only empty air as the disk flew onto its target.

Impact! The disk hit the gears above the vat head on, freezing them solid and stopping the tilt. The vines snaked back up to the vat but recoiled violently when they touched the ice.

Vakama took the hint. He launched another disk at one of the vines. When it struck, veins of frost began to travel the length of the blackened tendril. The other vines writhed frantically in the air, then all of them retreated back through a crack in the ground.

The Toa Metru of Fire let out a long sigh of

relief. The forge was safe, and more importantly, he had learned that Morbuzakh hated the cold. He was puzzling over what that might mean when the control room attendant came rushing over.

"That was . . . amazing!" said the Ta-Matoran. "I thought we had seen the last of the Toa when Lhikan disappeared. If you hadn't been here —"

"I did what I had to do," said Vakama quietly. He wasn't used to being seen as a hero and wasn't sure if he would ever feel comfortable about being one. "What happened? I thought that the vats never stopped moving."

"Come and see," said the attendant grimly. Vakama followed him into the forge control center. The foreman pointed to an ugly burn on one of the panels. "That's what happened. Some four-legged monster broke in and fried the controls with a burst of energy."

Vakama knelt down for a closer look. Some components had been damaged, but they could be repaired. That was not half as interesting as the scattered protodermis dust he saw on the floor near the damaged portion. He had seen dust like that once before, on a visit to Po-Metru, but this glittered in the light. It was only upon closer examination that he spotted the crushed Ko-Metru knowledge crystals mixed in with the dust.

The Toa Metru glanced up at the attendant. "I think I can fix this, if you can do a favor for me. I'm looking for a mask maker named Nuhrii. He wasn't at his home or at his forge. Have you seen him?"

"Yes. He was here this morning," the attendant replied. "He was looking for a Great Mask he made. It was tossed as flawed, but he said someone told him the mask was fine. He wanted to retrieve it before it went into the furnace for meltdown."

"Did he find it?"

"It's not here. Must still be on the reject pile, so I sent him over there. Nuhrii was talking pretty crazy, though. Said if he couldn't find the mask, he knew where there was a Kanoka disk that could make the greatest mask anyone had ever worn. I guess he's been working a little too hard."

"Yes, I guess so," Vakama replied, not at all convinced Nuhrii was crazy. More likely, the Matoran was walking into a trap — or getting ready to spring one.

The Toa of Fire thought hard as he walked. The walls of Nuhrii's home had been lined with tablets, souvenirs of his work. Each tablet showed an image of a Kanohi mask and the Kanoka disk from which it had been made. One of the tablets had been smashed on the floor, and a failed attempt made to put it back together.

The forge attendant had said Nuhrii had made a flawed mask. Vakama guessed it was the tablet featuring that mask that had been broken in anger. When Nuhrii heard the mask was in fact perfect, he tried to put the tablet back together before rushing off to find the Kanohi.

That still left a few questions. Who had discovered the mask was still a good one and notified Nuhrii? And was the note the Matoran had received the truth or simply bait to lure him into a trap?

Vakama hoped to find the answer at the huge, fenced-in lot just ahead. Its official name was Protodermis Reclamation Center, but to every mask maker in Ta-Metru, it was a graveyard. No matter how many hours of work had gone into a mask, a single, tiny flaw could ruin it. Then it would be transported here, to sit on top of a pile of other broken, useless masks until it could be fed to the furnace and melted down. It was the one place no mask maker ever wanted to visit.

A single guard stood at the gate. The bored look on his face disappeared when he saw a Toa coming toward him. "Who are you?" he asked.

"I am Toa Vakama." It felt so strange to say it. "Toa Metru of Fire. I need to get inside."

"I'm sorry, but I have orders from Turaga Dume. No one is allowed in. I don't want trouble with the Vahki."

"But you let Nuhrii in, didn't you? He's in danger, and I have to find him. Please open the gate."

"I can't! I could lose my job."

Vakama frowned. This argument was taking too much time. The guard was obviously more afraid of the Vahki than he was of making a Toa angry. *And why wouldn't he be? No Toa would ever harm an innocent.*

"Then I will open it for you," the Toa of Fire said. Concentrating harder than he ever had in his life, Vakama willed a narrow jet of flame from his hand. In an instant it had melted the lock into slag. "You did your job. Now I have to try and do mine."

The yard was quiet. Vakama walked past piles of Kanohi masks and other artifacts, all waiting behind the fences for their time in the Great Furnace. Some looked perfect to the naked eye, their flaws visible only to a truly skilled crafter. Others were badly mangled.

So focused was he on scanning the damaged items that he almost tripped over something in his path. When he regained his footing, he saw it was a Mask of Shielding someone had left lying in the path. Vakama bent down and picked it up. It looked familiar somehow, but he couldn't quite place it.

Then it struck him. The angle of the mask, the ridges around the eyepieces . . . these were marks of Nuhrii's work. Was this the mask the Matoran had been seeking, now cast aside as if it were worthless?

"Everyone seems to want that Kanohi today," said a Matoran behind him. Vakama turned to see the reclamation center caretaker approaching. "Nuhrii was here looking for it just a short while ago."

"But he didn't take it with him?" asked Vakama. "Why not?"

"Look for yourself. That mask has a hairline crack in the base," the caretaker replied, pointing to a barely visible flaw. "I've been doing this so long I can spot a bad one from a long way away. Mask maker must have cooled it too fast. Anyway, Nuhrii took one look at it, threw it down, and left. He was muttering something about forging the most powerful Kanohi ever made and showing up some other crafter. Vakama, I think his name was."

Me? Why would he want to outdo me? Vakama thought. *Sure, I had fewer masks wind up here, and Turaga Dume did ask me to craft a special Kanohi for him. But I never knew Nuhrii would be so jealous of that. After all, I learned so much from him.*

"I guess masks aren't the only things that can hide their flaws," the Toa of Fire said. "Do you have any idea where he's gone?"

The caretaker handed over a tablet. "He dropped this on his way out."

Vakama's eyes flew across the stone. There was no signature on the note, just some smudges of liquid protodermis. It read:

Nuhrii,

Come to the abandoned mask maker's house in the northern reaches. You'll learn a valuable secret there — how to turn a Great

Disk into a Kanohi mask that will live in legend. Come alone. Tell no one.

Vakama's mind reeled for a moment. He could see Nuhrii surrounded by shadowy tentacles that were reaching for him, grabbing him, squeezing the breath from the Matoran. Somehow, the Toa knew this danger was real, and it was happening now!

The caretaker watched Vakama race off and shook his head. Then he turned to the pile of broken masks and said, "Everyone's in such a hurry. Everyone except me . . . and all of you. We're in no rush to get where we're going, right?"

The Matoran laughed then, but Vakama was too far away to hear.

The Toa of Fire scanned his surroundings. He couldn't believe anything could make Nuhrii come here. This was a place no Ta-Matoran ever wandered, not if they hoped to see the twin suns rise again.

This had once been one of the most active sections of Ta-Metru. Vakama could remember riding the chutes here to see friends just a short time ago, but it seemed like ages had passed. Now the whole neighborhood was desolate and abandoned, surrendered to the power of the Morbuzakh. Half the buildings were reduced to rubble, and the rest did not look much better.

Vakama walked carefully, avoiding the chunks of solid protodermis that littered the street. Only the skittering of little Rahi among the wreckage broke the silence. Most of the Matoran who had lived here had fled, finding refuge with friends in the heart of the metru. Those who had chosen to stay were never seen or heard from again. Turaga Dume had declared the whole area off-limits, but soon found he did not need to dispatch Vahki to guard the place. No Matoran wanted to travel here.

Except Nuhrii, Vakama reminded himself. *But even if he is here, I may be too late to save him.*

As if in answer, a voice shouted, "Help!" It came from an abandoned crafter's home farther down the street. Vakama broke into a run, then stopped short when he saw the twin Morbuzakh vines slithering toward the same building. They were moving too quickly. He could never hope to outrace them.

"Help!"

Vakama loaded his last disk into the launcher and hoped he was making the right decision. He had never used this particular kind of disk before or even forged a mask from one. Its power was the least predictable and might make a bad situation worse. But there wasn't any other choice.

The disk shot through the air and struck the first vine, then began a sweeping arc that would bring it back to Vakama. On its way, it clipped the second vine, just as the Toa Metru had hoped it would. Before his eyes, both vines began to shimmer and fade. Then they were gone, teleported somewhere else in Metru Nui. Vakama hoped he had not just created a greater danger for someone else to deal with.

The door to the house was unlocked. As

soon as it was opened, a cloud of protodermis dust flew out, blinding and choking Vakama. When he could see again, he discovered the way in was blocked by rubble.

"Who's there? Help me! I'm trapped back here!" It was Nuhrii's voice, coming from somewhere beyond the pile of protodermis. The Morbuzakh vines had brought down the roof and were no doubt getting ready to start on the walls when the Toa Metru showed up.

For a moment, Vakama considered using his elemental power to melt through the obstacle. But his powers were so new, he had too little control over them. Make a mistake and the whole district might burn. No, he would have to do it the hard way, block by block.

Vakama removed one chunk of protodermis, but when he took out a second, the rubble shifted and more fell from the roof. "Hey, watch it!" Nuhrii shouted. "What are you trying to do?"

Vakama began again, proceeding more carefully. He shifted a block, paused, shifted it some more, until he was certain it wouldn't cause a collapse. It took a lot of careful work, but he finally managed to create a big enough opening for Nuhrii to crawl through. The Matoran was coated in dust but did not seem hurt.

"I thought I would never get out of there," said Nuhrii. Then he looked up at his rescuer for the first time. "Vakama! You!"

"Are you all right? What were you doing here?"

"Okay, why shouldn't I tell you? I came here to learn how to turn a Great Disk into a Mask of Power you could never dream of making. Then I would be the one others came to for the important Kanohi."

In all the time Vakama had worked as a mask maker, he had never once raised his voice. It had been Nuhrii who first hired him as a mask-making apprentice, and Nuhrii who had taught him the basic skills. But now, as Vakama thought of all he had been through to find the Matoran, he felt anger rise in him.

"Look around you, Nuhrii," the Toa said harshly. "Look at what the Morbuzakh has done to our city! This is no time to be thinking of personal glory. Everyone has to work together to stop this menace. That Great Disk you have is the key to saving Metru Nui. I don't know how, but it is. You have to tell me where to find it!"

Nuhrii looked shocked. It took him a moment before he could speak, but when he did, his tone was that of a Matoran ashamed. "The Great Disk? I — I didn't know. Yes, I will gladly help you find it."

The two left the house and started walking out of the abandoned zone. Although Nuhrii spoke under his breath, Vakama could hear him saying, "We'll get the disk. We'll stop the Morbuzakh. And everyone will know that I saved Metru Nui!"

The Toa Metru of Fire could only shake his head and walk on.

Whenua stood before the south gate of the Onu-Metru Archives, about at the end of his patience. "All right. For the fourth time, I am Whenua. I worked here my whole life. I need to get inside and find Tehutti before he does something we are all going to regret a whole lot."

He waited for an answer from the gate guard, who did not look impressed by the sight of a Toa Metru of Earth. Whenua considered finding another access to the Archives, but given that they covered almost the entire metru, it could be a long chute ride to another gateway. And there was no guarantee the guard there would be any more cooperative.

"Okay, you look like a Toa," said the guard. "But not any Toa I've ever seen. And Whenua? Whenua is an archivist, and he sure doesn't carry twin drills like yours. If you don't want to give me your real name, fine, but I can't let just anyone in here."

Whenua did his best to hold his temper. It would take too long to explain about how artifacts called Toa stones transformed six Matoran into Toa Metru, even assuming the guard would believe that. Even more frustrating was the fact that his Great Mask of Power might prove a help here, but he didn't even know what that power might be yet.

"Can you at least tell me if Tehutti is here?"

The guard chuckled. "Tehutti's always here, Toa 'Whenua.' He spends his whole life down with the exhibits. He showed up here all excited about some shipment or another, probably another Rahi only its mother could love. But there's nothing on the ship schedule for today."

Whenua frowned. When he had first found out Tehutti was missing, he went to the archivist's home. There he found a note offering an exotic Rahi for the Archives in exchange for a Great Disk. The note featured a crude drawing of the Rahi and was signed by a Ga-Metru Matoran named Vhisola. From the sound of things, Tehutti had rushed right over to make the exchange.

The Toa Metru of Earth made his decision. He pushed past the guard and went to the doorway. "Call the Vahki if you want to, I have to get in there. Now where did they hide those levers today?"

While the guard protested, Whenua ran his hands over the surface of the doorway. The Archives boasted a unique security system. Each door had three hidden levers whose location was changed every day. They had to be thrown in the right combination for the door to open, and that changed every day, too. Every Onu-Matoran believed it to be the perfect protection against intruders.

"Go ahead," said the guard. "No one has ever made it past that door. You won't stand a —"

Whenua threw the levers, one, two, three. The great door opened with a hiss. The Toa of Earth turned toward the guard and said, "What was that? Couldn't hear you over the door opening."

* * *

To Whenua, the Onu-Metru Archives were more than a storehouse or a museum. In his eyes, they were more magnificent than the crystal Knowledge Towers of Ko-Metru, the Great Temple, and the sculpture fields of Po-Metru all put together. The main floors extended for a great distance in every direction, and when they had taken up most of the space in the metru, work had begun on the lower levels and subbasements. The Archives now occupied the subterranean depths of the city, extending far beyond the boundaries of Onu-Metru.

Nor could it be said that the Archives were "finished." As more exhibits were added, Onu-Matoran workers continued to dig deeper and deeper down to find space to house them. Over time, they and the archivists had become so accustomed to the dim light underground that the brightness of the twin suns was hard on their eyes.

On the outside, the Archives looked grim and imposing. Inside, it was a vast treasure trove of every creation that had ever walked Metru

Nui. Rather than the dry historical records and prophecies of Ko-Metru, this was a living museum. Every Rahi beast, every insectlike Bohrok, every creature in the Archives was part of a living record. Inside their protodermis stasis tubes, they were alive but suspended in time forever.

Whenua walked into the first of the Rahi wings, enjoying the familiar scents of the Archives. He nodded a greeting to one of the oldest exhibits, a Nui-Rama captured in flight whose stasis chamber hung from the ceiling high above. All around, archivists scurried back and forth pushing their transport carts. These were used for moving exhibits of all sizes through the subterranean, protodermis-lined tunnels.

Whenua turned and headed for Tehutti's pride and joy, an exhibit of a Kane-Ra bull. Before he had even walked through the archway, he could see something was wrong. The section looked like a live Rahi had passed through, shattering the display case and scattering artifacts. Fortunately, only the outer shell had been broken. Had the inner casing been cracked, the Rahi inside might well have come to life again and rampaged through the Archives.

Whenua spotted Tehutti's transport cart in a corner, empty. Lying near it was a hammer, the kind used in Ta-Metru forges. The archivist in Whenua was dismayed. Ta-Metru artifacts belonged on one of the sublevels, not in a Rahi section. It was only when he looked again at all the damage that he realized why the hammer was there.

Who would want to sabotage these relics? he wondered. *Someone from Ta-Metru? Why?*

Shrugging, Whenua moved on to the next exhibit hall. Here were more Rahi, even larger ones, and carvings of those that had either eluded capture or whose displays had been moved into storage. The Toa Metru of Earth was looking for anything out of place, when one carving caught his eye. It depicted a massive Rahi with four legs and a long, muscular tail, ideal for striking out at opponents. Carved underneath the picture were the words "Nui-Jaga. Found in Po-

Metru, near the Sculpture Fields." Beside that was the name of the carver, Ahkmou.

A Nui-Jaga, he thought. *A Po-Metru Rahi. But this is the same beast Vhisola offered in trade for the Great Disk!*

As an archivist, Whenua was skilled at starting from the present and working back. No Ga-Matoran would even know what a Nui-Jaga was, most likely, let alone have one captive to trade. The offer to Tehutti had been a fake, probably written by someone other than this Vhisola. It was bait to get Tehutti to the Archives so the Great Disk could be stolen from him!

That thought made him realize something even worse. Whoever was trying to get the Great Disks — possibly that four-legged hunter Vakama talked about — might be right here in the Archives, planning an ambush. For a moment, he wondered if he should try to find help. Maybe a Toa, or even the Vahki . . .

Then he remembered — he *was* a Toa. It was his job to face danger and overcome it. And nothing — *nothing!* — would make him risk the safety of his Archives or his city.

He ran for the nearest exit to the outer dock. Still getting used to his new, far more powerful form, he stumbled a few times and almost crashed into a display of parasitic krana. With a shudder, he kept going, thanking the Great Beings he had not set those *things* loose.

Any shipment, no matter how large or small, had to come through the outer dock. The Matoran who worked here were both smart and brave. It was their job to make sure every "exhibit" was ready to be placed in a stasis tube, where its life processes would be slowed to a crawl. If one of the creatures intended for archiving decided to wake up, it would be up to the dockworkers to put it back to sleep again.

When Whenua arrived on the dock, a four-Matoran crew was trying to subdue a Gukko bird long enough for it to be put in stasis and archived. The powerful winged beast was objecting. There was about a fifty-fifty chance it would break away and head for the sky, carrying a Matoran or two with it.

Whenua went over to help, but the dock leader got in the way. "We have to do it ourselves," said the Matoran. "Understand? If we start depending on a Toa, what happens when you're not around?"

Whenua looked from the dock leader to the crew and back again. Then he nodded. "Okay, then — for now. Have you seen Tehutti?"

"He was headed for the next dock over. I told him not to waste his time. This Rahi was a last-minute find, but there aren't any others on the schedule. And nothing from any Vhisola."

"I know. I'm pretty sure he knows, too," replied Whenua, turning away. "Make sure that Gukko's fast asleep. Last time one got loose, it brought down half the exhibits in sublevel three."

"How did you know about that?" the dock leader asked. But the Toa of Earth was already gone.

* * *

Whenua pounded around the corner. All he could think about was finding Tehutti in time and stopping him from doing something the whole city would regret later. He scanned for any sign of the Matoran or for signs of a trap.

What he found was a well-concealed hole with a narrow ladder leading down into darkness. On a hunch, he began to climb down. He had made it about halfway when a rung gave way beneath his foot.

The next thing he knew, he was falling. And falling. Down, down, into the sublevels and sub-sublevels of the Archives, and then farther still, thinking to himself all the while: *Stupid. Stupid, stupid, stupid!*

Thoughts rushed through his mind. Was this the trap set for Tehutti, and had the Matoran already fallen into it? Just how far down did this pit go? And could even a Toa survive such a plunge?

Whenua found out an instant later, when he came to a crashing halt far below the lowest levels of the Archives. Despite spending a lifetime working here, even he had never been this far down before. But he had heard rumors of a level far below the surface, where exhibits that had proven potentially dangerous were placed for safekeeping.

The Toa Metru of Earth sat up and groaned. His bruises had bruises and his head was pounding. With a great deal of effort, he rose.

The hallways down here were even darker and more narrow than the ones above. Lightstones were few and far between. Anyone who came down here left in a hurry, so why waste illumination?

He had only taken three steps when he heard the sound every archivist dreads. It was a unique crunch, the sound of stasis-tube fragments being crushed underfoot.

Whenua forced himself to remain calm. *So one of the cases was broken, so what? Maybe it's only the outer shell that was damaged, and there's nothing to worry about. Yes, it had to be the outer shell, because if it was the inner shell, then something would be loose down here. Something very nasty.*

He had seen it happen before. Outer shells could take all kinds of pounding, but if the inner shell of a stasis tube cracked even a little, the rush of air would wake up the contents. When the contents had teeth, claws, and a hatred of being caged up, this generally turned out to be a bad thing.

Whenua did his best to move quietly down the corridor, not easy with his large frame. He reminded himself that he had been an experienced Onu-Metru archivist before becoming a Toa. As a Matoran, he had faced down his share of snarling Rahi. What could be down here that could possibly bother him now?

The answer came with twin beams of pure, blazing heat that creased the side of his Kanohi mask. The wall of the corridor sizzled where they struck, and the hallway was suddenly filled with the smell of charred protodermis. Whenua whirled to see a Rahkshi heading right toward him, red eyes gleaming in its hideous yellow face.

Startled, he found he could not remember the creature's exact name. But he didn't have to strain to recall its power — heat vision, capable of burning a hole through anything, including newly created Toa. No one was quite certain just where Rahkshi came from, but everyone wished they had stayed there.

Whenua ducked another heat blast and darted into another corridor. He needed time to think and space to maneuver, neither of which the Rahkshi was likely to give him. This would be a great time to use his Kanohi Mask of Power, if only he knew what it did. The twin earthshock drills he carried could punch their way through almost anything, and his elemental power . . .

Yes, that was it. When he reached the far end of the hall, he activated the drills and began tearing up the flooring. His elemental power would affect the earth underneath, but there was no harm giving it a little help.

The Rahkshi turned the corner and started toward him, its powerful body gleaming in the dim light. He could hear the horrible screech of the kraata it carried inside. Twin shafts of red shot toward him from the Rahkshi's eyes, Whenua barely moving aside in time. Then it was the moment to go to work.

The Toa Metru looked down and did his best to ignore the advancing creature. He willed the earth to rise, to form an impenetrable wall between him and the Rahkshi. He could see the soil beginning to shift, running together and then swirling as if mini cyclones had taken hold.

It was a toss-up who was more shocked by what happened next, the Rahkshi or Whenua. A mound of earth suddenly rose from the floor, hardening rapidly and blocking the creature from coming closer. Whenua took a step back and smiled, imagining how the other Toa would feel when he told them about this. Nuju probably couldn't even manage an icicle, or Onewa move a pebble, or . . .

The celebration came to an abrupt end. Twin red spots appeared on the earth wall, glowing brighter and brighter every moment. While Whenua had been patting himself on the back, the Rahkshi was focusing its power to melt the obstacle in its path.

Okay, maybe I won't tell the others about this, Whenua decided.

He ducked into a doorway just as the wall crumbled. There was something Tehutti had said about yellow Rahkshi once, if only he could remember. What was it? Tehutti was always on about one piece of exhibit trivia or another.

Then it came to him. Right after it uses its heat beams, the Rahkshi's eyesight is weakened temporarily. Tehutti had been right, too, for the creature walked right past Whenua's hiding place without spotting him.

Once the Rahkshi was gone, Whenua fought a strong urge to get out of the Archives. Then he remembered that Tehutti might well be down here, and if he was, the Rahkshi would find him. Like it or not, he had to go on.

But maybe I don't have to fight the Rahkshi, he realized. *Not if I can get something else to do it for me.*

Whenua raced down the hallway, stopping only long enough to pry a lightstone out of the wall. By its beam, he was able to spot the shattered Rahkshi stasis tube. He scooped up as many of the inner casing fragments as he could find, then went back on the trail of the creature.

As he walked, he tried to remember everything he could about this level. Over time, he had seen a number of exhibits sent down here, even marked a few for storage himself. If he was correct, all he had to do was find the right one.

It took a lot of walking, numerous twists and turns, and a few potentially dangerous mistakes before Whenua spotted the door he wanted. It was one of the few down here that had a sign, which read DANGER: MUAKA PEN. He could hear the great Rahi cat pacing and growling behind the door. Food was sent down to it once a day from the upper levels through a small chute, but Muaka were notorious for always being hungry. Better still, they did not get along with Rahkshi at all.

Whenua took a deep breath. This was going to be tricky. First, he scattered the protodermis fragments on the floor in front of the door. Then he used his earthshock drill to punch a hole through the lock. He waited until he could hear the Muaka charging before he dove for cover.

The door crashed open. The huge Rahi snarled, sniffing the air and snapping its massive jaws together. Whenua watched anxiously as the Muaka lowered its head and picked up the scent off the fragments. The beast's eyes narrowed at the smell of Rahkshi, and it took off at a run.

Whenua followed. Letting another creature loose down here went against his nature as an archivist, but it would be easier to cage the Muaka again than a Rahkshi. He just had to hope the Muaka found the Rahkshi before either found Tehutti.

He was deep in the heart of the storage level when he heard the snarls up ahead. The sounds were followed by red flashes of heat vision, then an impact that shook the entire section. The Muaka had tracked down his prey.

Whenua rounded the corner to see Rahi and Rahkshi locked in a mighty struggle. Ordinarily, the Rahkshi would be the clear favorite, but the Muaka's bulk reduced his foe's room to maneuver. Beyond them, the Toa could see an open chamber where Tehutti strained to get out from under a pile of artifacts.

The Toa forced himself to wait for the right moment. When Muaka lifted his right forepaw to strike, Whenua dove, slid across the floor past the two creatures, and ended up in the same chamber as the Matoran.

"Get me out of here!" Tehutti cried. "I'll do anything!"

Whenua worked quickly and carefully, pushing the debris aside and hoping the struggle outside would go on a little longer. "Anything? Then how about giving me that Great Disk you have while there's still a city up above to save."

Tehutti shrugged off the last few pieces of Metru Nui history and nodded. "I never thought I would be glad to see you. I fell down here, and some four-legged Rahi bait demanded I give him the disk. When I wouldn't do it, he brought this stuff down on me and left me here. You want the disk? You can have it. I'd rather be trapped in a broken chute with a horde of Vahki than hold on to it now!"

Whenua glanced out into the hall, made sure Rahi and Rahkshi were still busy, then slammed the door and locked it. "We'll have to dig a new tunnel to get out of here. In the meantime, you can explain why you ever thought a Ga-Matoran would have a Nui-Jaga to trade for the disk."

Tehutti watched in awe as Whenua's earthshock drills went to work on the wall. "I — I knew she wouldn't. My friend Ahkmou told me all about Nui-Jaga long ago, so I knew they didn't come from Ga-Metru. I wanted to see why someone wanted the Great Disk . . . and if they really did have a Nui-Jaga, well . . ."

"You would have traded the city's safety for a new exhibit to put your name on," Whenua replied.

"With you for a Toa Metru, Whenua, how safe is the city now?" Tehutti said. "Besides, nothing very bad is going to happen to Metru Nui. Turaga Dume will figure out some way to deal with the Morbuzakh and everything will be fine."

"I hope so." Whenua powered down his drills. He had managed to punch a good-size hole in the wall. On the other side was another darkened corridor with a distinct upward slope. Hopefully, it led to the main floors.

"Let's go," said the Toa of Earth. "We have a long journey ahead. If we run into the Morbuzakh, make sure to tell it that it's not a threat. I've never seen a plant laugh before."

The Matoran put down his tools and stood very still. He had heard two sets of footsteps behind him, heavy footsteps, and he really did not want to turn around and see who it might be.

"Well, well, well," hissed a too-familiar voice. "Here I am again."

The Matoran forced himself to look. Yes, it was Nidhiki again, this time accompanied by a hulking brute with energy crackling from his hands.

"I came back to get the Great Disks," Nidhiki continued. "You know, the ones I want *very badly*? The ones you promised to get for me?"

"I — I don't have them. Not yet," the Matoran stammered. "But I'll get them! It's just taking a little more time than I thought."

"I see," Nidhiki replied. He gestured with one of his legs, and his lumbering companion moved toward the Matoran. "This is my friend. He doesn't like Matoran. He particularly doesn't like you."

The Matoran looked up at the bestial face of the brute who towered over him. "I'm doing my best! Really!"

"Your best?" Nidhiki repeated. "Three of the Toa are close to finding the Great Disks. Your efforts to trap the Matoran and divert the Toa Metru have been failures. Do you know what that means?"

The Matoran swallowed hard as the two creatures crowded close to him. "N-n-no."

"It means you're going to do better than your best. I've been to Ko-Metru and arranged to keep Toa Nuju busy. I expect you to arrange a little surprise for Toa Matau and get the Le-Metru disk. I know you aren't foolish enough to disappoint me again, are you?"

The Matoran shook his head. He wanted to say something, but his mouth didn't seem to be working.

"Good. Then I hope the next time I see you, you will have all six Great Disks for me. But either way," Nidhiki added smiling, "it will be the last time I see you, Matoran. Understand?"

The two left before the Matoran could answer. They were barely out the door before he gathered up his things and headed for the chute station. He had an appointment in Le-Metru that he wouldn't miss if his life depended on it.

And it sounds like it does! the Matoran thought as he dashed out into the street.

From high atop a gleaming Knowledge Tower, Nuju looked down upon the landscape of Ko-Metru. For the Toa Metru of Ice, this was a most unusual vantage point. Normally, his eyes were on the sky, seeking to read the future from the brightness and movement of the stars.

But if Vakama was right, there might not be much of a future for Metru Nui if the Great Disks were not found. It was true that the Morbuzakh plant had done some pretty serious damage to the metru. Still, Nuju was not sure just how far he wished to trust the Toa of Fire's "visions."

Down below, all was still and silent. Even the hum of the transport chutes that carried Matoran from place to place was muted here. Nothing was allowed to disturb the work of the Matoran scholars who toiled in the crystal

Knowledge Towers. There they pored over the written records of Metru Nui, deciphered ancient prophecies, and crafted predictions of the future. Once, Nuju had been one of them. Now it was up to him to make sure there would be tomorrows to ponder.

At first, it seemed like that would be a simple enough task. The Ko-Metru Matoran who Vakama claimed had knowledge of the disk was named Ehrye. Finding him should not have been an issue. In fact, it was often impossible *not* to find Ehrye, even when you wanted to avoid him. He was constantly underfoot, running errands for different scholars and pleading for a chance to become one of them.

Nuju, naturally, had said no. Working in a Knowledge Tower required wisdom, patience, and experience. All Ehrye had to offer were enthusiasm and too much energy for his own good. So the Matoran went back to running errands and dreaming of life inside the towers.

And now, when I want *to find him, he's disappeared!* fumed Nuju.

A search of Ehrye's home had turned up a marked Ko-Metru chute station map and a disturbing journal entry. It read in part:

> *I'm going to show them. If I turn over the Great Kanoka Disk like I said I would, I'll learn a secret that will make them beg me to join a Knowledge Tower!*

Nuju shook his head. He had spent his whole life studying what might be and what would be in the days to come, and he knew one thing for certain. There was no future in what Ehrye was about to do.

The Toa of Ice leaped from the top of a Knowledge Tower, his eyes focused on the ledge of another. When he had maneuvered within arm's reach of it, he snapped a crystal spike from his back and swung it hard. It dug into the side of the tower. Nuju swung gracefully around the building, pulling the spike free as he did so. He repeated the exercise twice more on the way down, growing more used to his new Toa tools along the way. Someday, he knew, that experience might save his life.

Nuju had taken the chute map with him when he left Ehrye's house. He hit the ground close to the station that was marked on the map. The attendant was deep in thought and did not notice his approach.

"What? Oh!" he exclaimed when Nuju tapped his shoulder. "Who are you? What do you want?"

"I am Nuju, Toa Metru of Ice. I am looking for a runner named Ehrye. Have you seen him?"

The attendant frowned. "Yes, he was here. I saw him talking to a Matoran from another metru. I don't remember which. Then he jumped in a chute heading for one of the Knowledge Towers. He was muttering something about a disk."

"Where did he have this conversation?"

"Ummm . . . Let me see. I remember I was analyzing chute dynamics at the time and not really paying attention. But I think it was in that corner over there."

Nuju turned away without saying thank you. He was in no mood to waste words. Instead, he walked over to where the attendant had directed him and looked around. There was little to be seen, just a Po-Metru carving tool and a pass to the Onu-Metru Archives. Either might be important, or they might have been dropped by any of hundreds of Matoran who passed through this chute station.

The attendant had gone back to pondering. It was something Ko-Metru Matoran spent a lot of time doing, in hopes of one day securing a position in a Knowledge Tower. Unfortunately, it also made it hard to get their attention.

"If you see Ehrye again, hold on to him," Toa Nuju said.

"Hmmm? What? Hold on to whom?" the attendant asked, confused.

Nuju walked away, wondering why he even bothered to talk to some Matoran.

The chute Ehrye had taken led to the lower level of a Knowledge Tower. It was such a silent place it made the rest of the metru seem positively wild and loud. A small number of Ko-Matoran were hard at work, junior seers who hoped to one day ascend to the ranks of those who labored on the upper levels. Nuju had spent most of his life in Knowledge Towers and could not recall ever seeing a group of scholars looking so annoyed.

As usual, trying to get a scholar to take a break from his studies to talk was like trying to teach kolhii rules to a Rahkshi. They did not seem at all impressed by the presence of a Toa Metru. It was only when Nuju mentioned that a Great Disk was involved that one of them agreed to talk.

"A Great Disk, hmmm?" said the scholar. "Incredible power. I would love the chance to study one. Do you have it?"

"No, I am seeking it. I believe a Matoran named Ehrye is as well, and he may have come here."

"Ehrye!" the scholar spat. "So that was his name! He barged in asking a lot of questions about Kanoka disks, the Morbuzakh plant, and other things that were not his business. No, not his business at all! Then he took a chute to the top of the tower, which is forbidden!"

The other Matoran had turned to see what all the shouting was about. The scholar spotted their angry looks and dropped his voice almost to a whisper. "You will find him there, but you must do something for us in exchange for this information."

The scholar dug into his robes and pulled out a knowledge crystal a little larger than Nuju's hand. "The Morbuzakh vines have done great damage to our towers," the scholar explained. "With this crystal, a new tower can be grown. When you reach the top level, throw this into the air. Wherever it lands, a new tower shall appear."

Nuju took the crystal. "A gift to the future of Metru Nui, then. I will do it."

High atop the Knowledge Tower, the air was crisp and clean. One could always find a sense of peace and the time for contemplation here.

What could not be found, at least today, was any sign of Ehrye.

Toa Nuju felt the weight of the crystal in his hand. He approached the edge of the tower, took a deep breath, and tossed the crystal out into space. It tumbled through the air, vanishing into the mist below. An instant later, Nuju followed.

As he fell, he let doubt creep into his mind again. What if Vakama was wrong? What if the Great Disks proved to no one that they were Toa? What if the Great Disks didn't exist at all but were just legends? What then?

Nuju twisted his body in midair. He could barely see the outlines of the new tower. An instant later, he landed feetfirst on the top of the rapidly growing structure. It lifted him high in the air once more as it took its place among the other monuments to knowledge in Ko-Metru.

From this new vantage point, Nuju scanned the metru. Off to the west, he spotted something that looked out of place. A Knowledge Tower's rooftop was littered with protodermis blocks.

Since towers were grown, not built, there was no reason any construction material would be there.

He was about to dismiss it as one more strange thing in a city that seemed to be filled with them when he spotted movement behind the blocks. It was Ehrye! Nuju had barely realized that when he saw something much more frightening — a huge crack traveling up the side of the tower. The whole structure was about to fragment and take the Matoran with it.

Nuju got a running start and leaped off the tower. Using his crystal spikes, he swung from one chute to the next as fast as he could. When he was almost on top of the tower, he let go and dropped.

For once, the Toa of Ice tried not to think about the future. If he pondered the possible consequences of what he was trying to do, he would never be able to do it. He waited until his fall had brought him almost parallel to the crack in the tower, then held out his twin spikes and focused his ice power through them. Thin streams of ice shot from the tools, welding the crack shut as he fell.

Now came the hard part. Most of the damage was repaired, but if he could not stop his fall, he would be an ex–Toa Metru very quickly. He spun, twisted, and dug one spike into the side of the tower. It carved a gash in the crystal and he continued to fall, desperately trying to hang on to the Toa tool. Finally, with the ground much too close for comfort, the spike held and he came to an abrupt stop.

No wonder we had to be chosen to be Toa Metru, he thought as he began the long climb to the top of the tower. *No one would ever volunteer for this job.*

Ehrye was still where Nuju had last seen him: trapped behind protodermis blocks at the very top of the tower. Worse, the blocks had not been stacked haphazardly. They were arranged, almost like a puzzle, in such a way that moving the wrong one would bring them all crashing down on the Matoran.

Nuju spent a long time staring at the blocks before he gently shifted one. Then he went back to analyzing the barricade. Ehrye, impatient, shouted, "Are you going to get me out of here? What are you doing?"

"Quiet," Nuju replied. "Someone did not want you walking away from this tower. But you are important to the future of Metru Nui, fortunately for you, so the Toa of Ice is going to get you out of what you have gotten into."

"Yes, I heard you were a Toa," said the Matoran grimly. "Now I'll never have a chance at a promotion."

The Toa Metru ignored him. This puzzle was highly intricate, but it was designed to defeat someone who could not think ahead. *They picked the wrong Toa then,* Nuju said to himself.

It took an agonizingly long time, but finally enough blocks were cleared for Ehrye to slip out. He stretched himself and looked up at his rescuer. "I suppose you're wondering how I got here?"

"Yes. You took many risks, Ehrye, and broke a number of laws. I should turn you over to the

Vahki and be done with it. But I need you. Or, rather, I need the Kanoka disk you have located."

"Why should I give it to you?" Ehrye replied. "That disk could be my ticket to a Knowledge Tower position."

Nuju gestured at the pile of protodermis blocks. "It was almost your ticket to a tomb. Think about the future, Ehrye."

The Matoran spent a few minutes doing just that. Then he said, "I get full credit for finding it? And no Vahki come knocking on my door?"

"Vahki don't knock," Nuju reminded him. "They smash doors down. And they keep smashing them down until they find the one you're hiding behind."

"You have a point," Ehrye agreed. "Even if I didn't have to worry about them, there's still that big Rahi breath that walled me up here."

Nuju and Ehrye headed for the chute that would bring them back down to ground level. Still shaken by his experience, Ehrye wouldn't stop babbling. "I know why you're looking for that disk, Toa Nuju. It's the root, right?"

"Root?"

"The Morbuzakh plant — it has a king root. I found that out when I was researching the Great Disk. Stop the root, you stop the spread of the plant. But you need all six disks to do it."

"Then you will come with me to see the other Toa Metru now," Nuju said.

"There are more of you?"

"And then we will go get the Great Disk."

"Oh, I'll tell you where it is. I'll even go with you. But you're going to have to retrieve it. From what I've learned, no one but a Toa Metru has a chance of getting that disk from its hiding place."

"I see," Nuju said.

"In fact," continued Ehrye, "I might not get the Knowledge Tower job. But if the Great Disk is as hard to get as I think it is, your job might be open soon, Toa of Ice."

Neither one of them laughed at Ehrye's little joke.

* * *

When they reached the ground, Nuju gestured for Ehrye to follow him. To the Matoran's surprise, they did not head for a chute station but for the alley behind the tower.

"Where are we going?"

"Knowledge Towers do not crack by themselves," said Nuju. "Well, sometimes they do, but this one did not. I am searching for the cause."

Ehrye trailed along behind as Nuju walked up and down the length of the alley. Along the way, the Matoran peppered him with questions. "What are you looking for? Does that mean anything? What does it feel like to be a Toa Metru? Do you think the Morbuzakh plant will wreck the whole city?"

"Enough!" Nuju snapped. "The future will bring the answers to your questions, but only if you stop speaking long enough to notice them."

"That's what you always say," Ehrye grumbled.

"When it stops being true, I will stop saying it," Nuju replied.

The Toa of Ice moved around to a shadowed portion of the tower. There, just below eye level, was the beginning of the crack that had threatened to bring the whole structure down. Peering closely at it, he looked for any sign of the tool that had been used.

What he found was something quite different. The edges of the damaged area were melted and fused. In many places, the crystal had turned black. No Matoran tool had done this. It was a surge of energy.

Troubled, Nuju knelt down to examine the ground. Crushed knowledge crystals littered the pavement. The Toa of Ice carefully sifted through them to reveal scrapings on the ground below. They were the marks of a four-footed being who had stood right in that spot while he no doubt set his trap.

Vakama was right, Nuju thought. *This time. But who is this monster? Why is he doing this? Is he working for someone else, or does he stand to gain somehow by all this damage?*

He rose and walked toward the mouth of

the alley, not saying a word to Ehrye. The Matoran kicked at the knowledge crystal fragments before following. His thoughts had gone back to the missed opportunity of the Great Disk. If he could have gotten his hands on it or maybe somehow tricked Nuju into getting it for him, Ko-Metru would have been at his feet. Now it would be back to running errands. Unless, of course, he could still find a way to get the disk after Nuju found it.

Ehrye was still pondering that happy thought when Nuju stopped short. The Toa of Ice bent down to pick up an artifact, but Ehrye could not make out what it was. After a moment, Nuju turned around and held the item out. It was a small, intricate carving.

"What's that?" Ehrye asked.

"I thought perhaps you could tell me," said Nuju coldly. "This came from Po-Metru. It's signed by Ahkmou the carver."

Ehrye shrugged. "So?"

"At the chute station, the attendant said he saw you talking with a Matoran before you left for the Knowledge Tower. He couldn't remember who it was, but I think I know. It was Ahkmou, wasn't it? That's why there was a Po-Metru carving tool in the station. He was careless . . . must have been in a big hurry."

"Okay, so it was Ahkmou," Ehrye replied. "We're friends. We play kolhii together sometimes. What does this have to do with —?"

"Listen to me," Nuju said, leaning in so close that Ehrye was chilled by his frigid breath. "We are not playing kolhii now. All of Metru Nui is at stake. Now, what did Ahkmou want?"

Ehrye broke and ran. Nuju frowned and used a minimal amount of elemental power to block the alley with a wall of ice. Stymied, the Matoran turned around.

"Wrong answer," said Nuju.

"All right. He said he wanted to carve replicas of the Great Disks as a gift for Turaga Dume. He wanted to know all about them and figured I could get information from the Knowledge Towers."

"Is that all he said?"

"Yes," Ehrye answered, his eyes on the ground.

Nuju could tell he was not revealing the whole truth, but there would be time to uncover it later. For now, they needed to return to Ga-Metru and meet with the other Toa. He turned and walked toward the chute station, confident that Ehrye would be wise enough not to try to run again.

"What are you going to do about that ice wall?" the Matoran asked. "Will it melt?"

"Eventually."

"Won't there be questions? I mean, how many Matoran know there's a Toa of Ice around?"

"It will give the scholars something to ponder," said Nuju. "And before all is said and done, all of Metru Nui will know that Toa Nuju has arrived."

Matau, Toa Metru of Air, knew all about chutes. He had been riding the transparent, magnetized protodermis tubes from place to place all his life, as had most Matoran. Living in Le-Metru, transport hub for the entire city, he had even had the chance to repair a chute or three in his time. He was quite proud of the fact that no one outside of his metru knew more about chutes than he did.

All of which made it even stranger that he was now hurtling out of control through a chute at a ridiculously high speed, heading for what would probably be a very dead end.

Outside the chute, the green-and-brown structures of Le-Metru were nothing but a blur. Matau whipped around a corner, heading for a busy junction and hoping he was not about to collide with some poor Matoran. For at least the tenth time, he tried to jump through the walls of the chute and exit. But he was thrown back yet again, slamming into the opposite wall and then picking up speed again.

I wanted to get there quick-fast, but not this quick-fast, he thought. He wasn't sure how anyone could manage to seal off the walls of a chute, or whether this affected the entire metru system or just the tube he was rocketing through.

But I can take a smart-guess. Fire-spitter was right. These disks must be important, and someone doesn't want me to find mine.

Matau's mind raced almost as fast as his body through the chute. The chutes ran throughout the city, but the densest concentration was in Le-Metru. They all fed into one another. If it was only this chute that had been tampered with, then it should be possible to steer into another at the junction.

"Possible. Not healthy-safe, but possible," he muttered.

First thing Matau had to do was slow down. He unhooked his twin aero slicers from his back and tried digging them into the walls of the chute to act as brakes. But whatever had made the chute resist exits also made it too tough for the slicers to pierce.

I'm thought-planning like a Matoran still, Matau told himself. *The tools aren't the power. I'm a Toa-hero. I'm the power!*

The Toa Metru of Air glanced ahead. The junction was rushing up toward him, and a transport cart was heading for it from a side chute. At the rate he was moving, he would slam right into the cart. But if he could use his power to slow just a little . . .

Matau was not famous for deep thought and concentration, but he managed some now. He forced his will on the air in the chute, making it form a thick cushion to lower his speed. Little by little, he could feel himself slowing, but would it be enough?

The transport cart shot through the junction. A split second later, Matau went through. Straining, he reached out and grabbed the back of the cart, letting it pull him down the side chute.

The abrupt stop and change of direction almost ripped his arm out of the socket, but somehow he found the strength to hang on. It was only when he had traveled some way from his original chute that he let go and exited out the wall. Then he waited until the world around him stopped going in circles.

Toa Matau found himself not far from his original destination: the Ussal crab pen of the Le-Matoran named Orkahm. He decided to skip a chute and instead take the sky route via the cables that hung everywhere in Le-Metru.

Ussal pens could be found all over the metru. The carts they pulled transported goods too large or fragile for the chutes or carried Matoran who preferred to travel a little more slowly. The large crabs were specially trained to obey the commands of their riders, although they had been known to get temperamental at times. Even from high above, it was easy to locate an Ussal crab pen by the aroma — they were not the sweetest-smelling Rahi around.

Matau dropped to the ground near one of the crab keepers. "Don't worry-fear! It's me, Matau. I am a Toa-hero now!"

The keeper dropped his tools in surprise. "Wow! You've pulled some great jokes before, Matau, but this — this tops them all."

"This isn't a joke," Matau insisted. "I was given this Toa stone, and I brought it to the Great Temple, and . . . There isn't time for this. I am looking to seek-find Orkahm. Have you seen him?"

"No," the keeper said. "And I would just as soon he stays away. He's been acting crazy. Said he found something on his route-path, but wouldn't show it to anyone. He was going to bury-hide it. Orkahm always seemed like such a good rider. Who knew the pressure would get to him?"

Matau nodded. It would take too long to explain the situation, but he knew Orkahm had not lost his mind. The Matoran had found a Great Disk and knew someone would try to take it away from him, maybe the same someone who had sabotaged the chute. "So he's gone?"

"He is, but his cart's here. Why are you so interested, Matau? Planning a trick-joke on him?" the keeper said, laughing. "He already doesn't like you. I don't think you want to make it worse."

Matau spotted Orkahm's cart, sitting alone off to the side of the pens. Each rider kept a log-book of his travels during the day, and Orkahm was no exception. Matau fished it out from under the seat and flipped it open, only to discover the careful rider had written the whole thing in code.

Matau was tempted to give up. Then he reminded himself that the other Toa Metru had probably made contact with their Matoran and were waiting for him. He couldn't show up empty-handed. Besides, finding Orkahm and the disk would prove to everyone in Le-Metru that he was a Toa-hero.

He sat down on the cart and began studying the code. Matau had known Orkahm a long time. The Matoran was thorough, cautious, and meticulous, which made him a slow rider. Matau, on the other hand, had always been fast and reckless, which was why the two never got along.

But the most important thing Matau remembered about Orkahm was that he had little imagination.

Once the Toa realized that, breaking the code was simple. Orkahm had substituted numbers for letters, but it wasn't done in a particularly clever way. Deciphered, there were three entries, all dated the day before.

Disk hidden.

A. wants disk.

Moto-hub sector 3.

He's deephiding in sector 3, Matau realized. *He's either a fool or very, very scared. Probably both.*

Matau jumped in a chute headed northeast. Sector 3 was just across one of the major protodermis canals from Ta-Metru. It had long been known for the sheer number of chute malfunctions that took place there. These were blamed on everything from poor construction to just bad luck, until repair crews sent to the area started disappearing. That was when rumors began to spread that the Morbuzakh was behind all the troubles. Since then, all repair crews traveled with

Vahki escorts. Even with that, the Vahki usually returned alone. And since the security squads were incapable of speech, they couldn't explain what had happened.

If Orkahm wanted a place to hide, he chose a dangerous one, Matau thought. *Unless he thinks-knows something I don't?*

Matau leaped out of the chute at a station on the outskirts of the sector. The area had not been abandoned. There were still plenty of riders and other Matoran to be seen, hard at work. But everyone seemed to be moving very quickly and looking over their shoulders every few seconds. This part of Metru Nui wasn't ruled by Turaga Dume or the Vahki. It was ruled by fear.

The sudden appearance of a Toa in their midst drew a lot of attention from the Le-Matoran. They crowded around, asking questions, admiring his armor, and saying that now they were sure everything would be all right. Matau was having such a good time he almost forgot why he was there.

He was reminded abruptly when a transport

manager came up to him and said, "Are you looking for Orkahm?"

"Yes. How did you know?"

"He came hurry-running through here a little while ago. He said someone might be following him, and if anyone asked, not to tell them where he had gone."

"Then why are you telling me? Not that I am sad-complaining," said Matau.

"Because you are a Toa," the transport manager replied. "I have seen Toa before, a long time ago, but never met one. I know the legends, though — how Toa are here to protect us and keep us safe. Whatever Orkahm is doing, I don't think he's safe right now. Do you?"

Orkahm had made straight for a long-unused chute that went even deeper into sector 3. Matau was about to follow when he noticed something on the support struts beneath the chute. Something had been scratched into the solid protodermis.

Matau knelt down to take a closer look.

The carving was relatively fresh, made with a short, sharp instrument. It had left behind protodermis dust in the scratchings, but not dust from the strut. This looked more like dust from Po-Metru. Carved into the strut was a single word: PEWKU.

Matau read it once more to make sure he wasn't mistaken. Under ordinary circumstances, he would have dismissed this as some Matoran's idea of fun, leaving a mark behind on a chute. Matau had done that sort of prank himself in the past, along with hundreds of others.

But this was no joke — this was a message. Pewku was the name of Orkahm's favorite Ussal crab, the one he had been riding for as long as Matau could remember. The Toa doubted Orkahm would have taken the time to scratch this in the strut.

Someone else, then, he said to himself. *As a code-sign?*

Without hesitating even for a moment, Matau jumped into the chute and began to follow the trail of the missing Matoran.

* * *

The farther one traveled into this portion of Le-Metru, the more the buildings, chutes, and cables seemed to crowd in. The residents were fighting a losing battle against the Morbuzakh here. It was obvious that even the Vahki were not venturing this far, because Matau spotted at least two nests of insectoid Nui-Rama on rooftops. Normally, they would have been netted and shipped off to the Archives long ago.

Matau could see the chute change direction sharply up ahead. To his trained eye, it was obvious that the chute had not been built that way. Someone had rerouted it and not done a very good job. Still, the cylinder of energy held as he tore around the corner and went flying into the air.

Of course. Badly fix-patched chute, cut-severed end . . . why am I surprised?

He landed hard amid a tangled nest of transport cables. These cables helped feed energized protodermis into the chutes and chute stations, not to mention being great fun to swing from. Matau was puzzling over how he would ever untangle them when he noticed something in the center of the tangle, looking like it had been caught in a Fikou spiderweb.

It was Orkahm!

"Rider!" Matau said. "How did you get yourself in this trap-snare?"

"I didn't! Someone put me here!" the Matoran replied. "Now, please get me out!"

Matau worked as quickly as he could, unknotting the cables but being careful not to tighten them around Orkahm in the process. When he was done, the Matoran practically fell into his arms.

"What happened?" Matau asked. "Where is the Great Disk?"

"Not here. I wish it was! I wish I could give it away right now, with all the trouble it has caused me," Orkahm said, his voice filled with exhaustion. "Ever since I found it, I've been followed by two beings, one huge, one with four legs, not to mention having Ahkmou on my back about it. Then I got this message."

He handed Matau a small tablet. It read:

The disk you found is vital to the security of the city. Bring it to Moto-Hub sector 3 and take the marked chute.

"But you didn't bring the disk," Matau said.

"I thought it might be a trick. Maybe they wanted to follow me to where it was hidden. No sooner did I get here than these cables snapped tight around me. I heard a voice say that someone would be along soon to talk to me. But no one came until you, Matau."

"You know who I am?" Matau said, surprised.

"Of course! Only you would be foolish enough, reckless enough, to come after me here. You were a danger to everyone on the road as a rider, and you will probably be a danger as a Toa, too. But thank you."

For the first time in his life, Matau found he had nothing to say. It was just as well, too, for if he had spoken he would never have heard the slithering sound coming from among the cables. He shot a look at the web only long enough to see three Morbuzakh vines working their way toward them.

"We have to get out of here!" he shouted.

Now Orkahm saw the vines, too, and was backing away. "How? The chute only goes in one direction, and it's too high up to jump to anyway. We're trapped!"

"Toa-heroes are never trapped," Matau said, doing his best to sound the way he imagined a Toa Metru should. He grabbed Orkahm and yelled, "Hang on!" as the twin aero slicers on his back began to whirl.

It wasn't easy getting off the ground with the extra weight of Orkahm, but they managed it with barely an inch to spare. The vines wrapped themselves around the chute struts and snaked their way after the two, but by now Matau was flying too high and too fast for them to catch.

"How did you know this would work?" Orkahm asked.

"I'm a Toa-hero. This is what we do," Matau answered. He decided it was best to keep to himself the fact that he'd had absolutely no idea whether the stunt would work and just took the chance.

Maybe that is what being a Toa-hero is really about in the end, he thought as he flew over Le-Metru. *Taking the chances you have to take. Doing the things no one else is able to do.*

Matau banked sharply and headed for the center of the metru. *I think I could get to like this,* he said to himself with a smile.

Onewa, Toa of Stone, ran at full speed through the Sculpture Fields of Po-Metru. Unfortunately, full speed was not all that fast. His new body was built for strength, not sprinting.

"I need a Mask of Speed," he muttered to himself. "If a Toa of Stone has to do this sort of thing, he needs whatever help he can get."

He pushed the thought of masks out of his mind. He had no idea what Mask of Power he was wearing, what it might do, or even how to make it work. He hoped that eventually that would change, but for now there was no point in worrying about it. Onewa had a mission to perform, so, legs aching and heartlight flashing rapidly, he kept running.

The Sculpture Fields were home to hundreds of statues, most of them far too big to fit in even the largest Po-Metru warehouse. Onewa's goal was one particular work of art, with a very unique feature: a Matoran named Ahkmou was sitting on top of it.

"Hey, Onewa," the Matoran shouted. "What gets harder to catch the faster you run?"

Onewa glared at him. "My breath! You can do better than that, Ahkmou."

"Well, hurry up and get me down from here!" the Matoran replied. "You can, can't you?"

"Just stay there. I'll get to you."

As he ran, the Toa of Stone thought back to how he had ended up here. His first stop had been Ahkmou's home, but the Matoran wasn't there. Carvings were scattered all over the floor, furniture was thrown about. Onewa worried that Ahkmou had been kidnapped.

A visit to his workplace had turned up no sign of him either. The other carvers said that their coworker had been jumpy lately, especially after he got a visit from two strangers. One had four legs, the other was a giant, and neither looked like he was bringing good news.

Onewa frowned. The description sounded a lot like the hunter Vakama claimed to have seen, although there was no telling who the brute with him might be. Still puzzling over that, he opened Ahkmou's carver desk. Inside, it was a jumble of items. Onewa spotted not only Po-Metru carving tools but equipment from Ta-Metru, maps from Le-Metru, and assorted items from other parts of the city. It wasn't illegal to have any of that, of course, but why would a Po-Metru carver need it?

Then again, maybe it all means nothing, Onewa thought. *The two strangers could have been some new kind of Vahki that Turaga Dume has put in service. The items in his station could be souvenirs of some kind. I mean, what are the chances Ahkmou has a Great Disk and hasn't told everyone he knows about it already? I don't think Vakama had a "vision." I think he was just seeing things.*

There were still questions to answer, though. Onewa had stumbled on a hidden map of the Sculpture Fields on his way here. One spot was marked, and it was the very same spot at which Ahkmou was waiting now. Who wanted him to go there? And why?

Onewa reached the base of the statue. It was a very long way to the top. Taking a deep breath, he dug his two new tools, called proto pitons, into the stone and began to climb.

Ahkmou leaned over the side and watched. Then he said, "So how did you do it? Really?"

"How did I do what?"

"Make yourself look like a Toa."

"I don't just look like a Toa," Onewa snapped. "I am a Toa!"

"Oh," Ahkmou said, so quietly Onewa could barely hear him. "I see. You must be one of the six, then. And you were looking for me? Is that why you came out here?"

Onewa dragged himself a little farther up the side of the statue. "Yes. I came out here because a fire spitter has been standing too close to his forge and told me I should. He said you had a Great Kanoka Disk."

Ahkmou shook his head. "I don't know anything about any disk. I'm a carver."

With one last effort, Onewa pulled himself to the top of the statue. He lay there, panting for a moment, before looking up at the Matoran. "So how did you get up here?"

Ahkmou stood up and backed away a few steps. Suddenly, he seemed nervous. "I — um — I just came up to . . ." The Matoran's eyes went wide. "Nidhiki!"

Onewa turned around just in time to catch a fleeting glimpse of a four-legged creature on the field below, vanishing behind a statue.

"Who is —" he began, looking back at Ahkmou. But the Matoran was gone. Onewa leaned over the side and saw Ahkmou climbing swiftly down on a series of spikes wedged into the statue.

"Hey! Come back here!" the Toa shouted, but Ahkmou was already leaping from statue to statue, heading for the exit from the field.

Onewa gave a growl of frustration and

started after him. He had just begun the climb down when he noticed something carved into the top of the statue. It read PO-METRU CHUTE 445.

All right then, Ahkmou, the Toa of Stone said to himself. *I may not be as fast as you, but now I know where you're going.*

Getting out of the Sculpture Fields would be a great deal harder than getting into them had been, that much Onewa was sure of. The ground between his location and the exit was unstable, thanks to years of tilling the soil to recycle protodermis. Half the statues were sinking, and the other half had already disappeared in the marshy ground. Normally, only hopping from one sculpture to another would make for a safe exit.

Onewa paused halfway down the makeshift ladder and began whirling his proto piton. "Toa don't hop," he said. "Not when they can do this."

As smoothly as if he had been doing it for years, Onewa slung the piton toward another statue. The edge of the sharp tool caught the stone and held. After testing it with a few tugs,

Onewa stepped off the climbing spikes and swung through the air.

He looped in a wide arc around the sculpture, even as he readied his other piton. At the apex of his swing, he tossed the second piton and watched it bite into another sculpture. "Yes!" he bellowed, smiling. "Who needs chutes? This is the way a Toa should travel!"

Ahkmou elbowed his way through the crowd at Chute Station 445. This was the busiest station in all of Po-Metru, linking as it did to all the other districts. Getting through it was a nightmare. Ahkmou knew that was most likely the reason he had been directed here. In this mob, anything could happen, and no one would ever notice.

Well, this is one Matoran who doesn't intend to mysteriously disappear, he thought. *I'm catching the next chute, and then let them try and find me.*

Ahkmou felt only one twinge of regret as he headed for the chute to Ta-Metru. He had hoped to somehow get his hands on the Po-Metru Great Disk before he left. But when Toa

Onewa showed up, running suddenly seemed like a better idea.

"At least I lost that big kolhii-head," he grumbled. Then he cast a quick glance back to make sure Onewa hadn't followed him. "Why anyone would make him a Toa, I can't —"

Still searching the crowd for Onewa, Ahkmou slammed right into a pair of pillars and fell over. He sat up, brushed himself off, and was about to snarl something about idiots putting pillars in the middle of a chute station when he noticed something very disturbing.

They weren't pillars. They were legs.

Toa Metru legs.

Ahkmou looked up into the smiling face of Onewa. "Going somewhere?" the Toa asked.

"Just — just back to work," Ahkmou stammered. "Can't, um, spend all day sitting on statues, you know."

"That's funny," Onewa replied, gesturing to the nearby chute. "I didn't know they had moved your carver's table to Ta-Metru."

The Toa reached down and gently grabbed

Ahkmou, lifting him into the air. "Why don't we try this again? Hello, Ahkmou. Where are you going? Why did someone leave a note for you on top of a sculpture? And where is the Great Disk?"

"I don't know what you're talking about! Put me down!" Ahkmou shouted.

Onewa noticed a Vahki responding to the disturbance. The crowd parted to let the security enforcer through. He considered just bolting with the Matoran, but sudden movement would be sure to provoke a pursuit, and there wasn't time for that.

For his part, Ahkmou had not even noticed the Vahki. His attention was riveted by the sudden appearance of Nidhiki, who was watching the action from a shadowy corner of the station with a sinister grin on his face. The Matoran frantically weighed the choice between an angry Toa or a smiling, four-legged hunter and found it wasn't any choice at all.

"Okay, tell you what," Ahkmou said quickly. "I'll help you find the Great Disk, but we have to go now. Understand? Now!"

Onewa glanced at the Vahki, who was still a short distance away. When he looked over his shoulder to make sure the other direction was clear, he spotted Nidhiki withdrawing into the shadows. The Toa's eyes narrowed at the sight of him.

"Sure, Ahkmou," Onewa said quietly. "I think I do understand."

"One of them is lying."

Vakama's words were hard, but his tone was very soft. The Toa were sitting in the shadow of the Great Temple, sharing the tales of their adventures. When the stories were finished, it didn't take a vision to know something was very wrong.

"What's that you're whisper-saying, fire-spitter?" asked Matau.

Vakama glanced at the six Matoran, who were standing off to the side and looking uncomfortable. "It's just — look at what happened. We went out looking for six Matoran, and each of them was gone. They were lured away and promised whatever they wanted most in return for a

Great Disk. Meanwhile, we ran into 'accidents' and sabotage every step of the way. Someone didn't want us to find them."

"And you think one of the Matoran betrayed the others?" asked Nuju. "What about that four-legged monster and his friend? Couldn't they be behind all of this?"

Vakama hesitated. Nokama leaned over and said, "Go ahead, Vakama. Tell us."

"I've seen the four-legged one before," Vakama said quietly. "His power and his rage were . . . frightening. I don't think he would bother with such elaborate methods to lure the Matoran. He would have just taken them."

"But which one can it be?" Nokama asked. "They all knew where to find a Great Disk. They all had reasons to dislike one of us. If anything, we have too many clues: notes from Ahkmou to Vhisola, notes from Vhisola to Tehutti, Ta-Metru tools, Le-Metru chute maps. Where do we start?"

"You are looking at what they have in common, Nokama," said Whenua. "When an archivist is trying to solve a mystery of the past, he looks for what is uncommon, out of place. What is different about one of them?"

Nuju frowned. "Old methods won't solve this, historian."

"No, Whenua has a point," said Nokama. "For example, each of the Matoran recognized us as Toa Metru. Someone must have told them we had transformed. But none of them ever referred to six Toa, did they? Each Matoran only seemed to know about the Toa from his or her own metru. So maybe —"

"You're wrong," cut in Onewa. "I didn't mention it before. I didn't think it was important. But when I talked to Ahkmou on top of the sculpture, he said something odd. He said, 'You must be one of the six.' And he seemed to know our four-legged friend. He called him by name — Nidhiki."

All eyes went to the Po-Matoran, who was standing apart from the others. "From what you said, Onewa, Ahkmou was the only one who lied about knowing the location of a Great Disk," said Nuju. "All the others practically bragged about it."

"Ahkmou's name was on the note to Vhisola," said Nokama.

"There was protodermis dust from Po-Metru near the sabotaged vat controls," said Vakama.

"Ahkmou was asking Ehrye about the Great Disks," added Nuju.

"Orkahm said Ahkmou need-wanted his disk very badly," said Matau.

"And Ahkmou knew about Nui-Jaga, enough to use the idea of one to lure Tehutti to the Archives," finished Whenua.

There was a long, uncomfortable silence, finally broken by Nokama. "Do you think . . . ? Why would he do that?"

"I say we ask him," said Onewa, rising. "And then we haul him to the Vahki."

"No!" snapped Vakama. "We mustn't!"

"Fire-spitter, I am getting tired of you giving orders," Onewa growled, taking a step toward the Toa of Fire. "Who made you leader? Maybe it's time we found out just which is more powerful, fire or stone!"

Nokama stood and placed herself between them. "Stop it! Metru Nui is in danger. This is no time to fight among ourselves!"

"If you had something besides rocks in your head, carver, you would understand," said Whenua. "Even if Ahkmou is the traitor, he is still the only one who knows where the Po-Metru disk is hidden. We need him. But if you feel like you can't keep an eye on him, well, I —"

"Listen, you dusty librarian, I found him, and I can keep him in line!" snapped Onewa. "At least until I have the Great Disk in my hands."

"Our job has just begun," said Nokama. "If Ahkmou has betrayed Metru Nui, he is a danger to us all, and so is that Nidhiki. Maybe they are working together, or maybe not, but we must beware of both."

"Or maybe they need to beware of us," answered Onewa.

"Nokama is right," said Vakama. "We have to find the Great Disks before it's too late. And we have to keep an eye on all the Matoran while we're doing it. The Morbuzakh is not our only enemy."

Their conversation was interrupted by the ugly sound of a protodermis structure snapping in two. They turned to see Morbuzakh vines hauling the broken remains of a small Ga-Metru temple into the sea.

"As if we need more than one, with that thing around," said Onewa. "Let's go. We have disks to find and a really nasty weed to rip out by the roots."

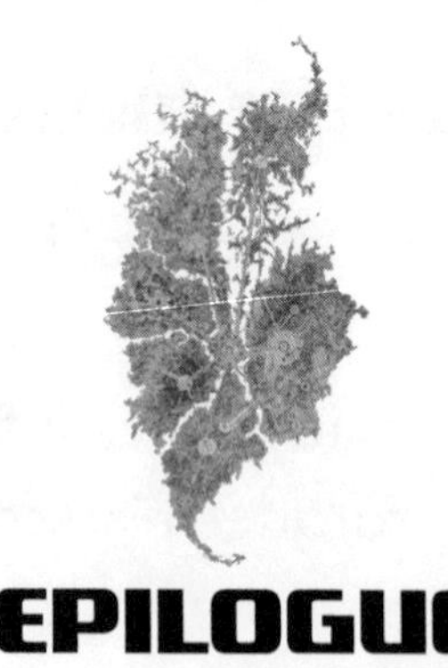

EPILOGUE

Turaga Vakama paused. The memories of his days as a Toa Metru were powerful ones. There were many times he thought he might never get the chance to tell the tales of Metru Nui and the struggle to save it. Now the words spilled from him like a flood, and he found it almost too much to bear. Toa Lhikan . . . the forges of Ta-Metru . . . his life as a Toa . . . all so long ago.

"That can't be the end of the story," said Takanuva, Toa of Light. "I mean, there is more, isn't there?"

Turaga Vakama smiled. "You were the Chronicler before you were a Toa, Takanuva, and that questioning spirit still lives on in you. Always you seek to know what is hidden. But you are right, that is only the beginning of my tale."

"Did you find the Great Disks?" asked Tahu Nuva. "Did you defeat the Morbuzakh? We must know!"

"And so you shall," said Vakama. "But I am weary, and there is much work still to be done. I will continue my tale tomorrow. Before I am done, you will know why we fought so hard for Metru Nui — and why we were forced to leave. Mata Nui, in his wisdom, brought us to this beautiful island that bears his name. But home will always be Metru Nui."

"Very well, then," said Gali, Toa Nuva of Water. "We will leave you for now, wise one. I know I feel the need for a long talk with Turaga Nokama, and I am sure my brothers have similar ideas."

"Indeed," answered Kopaka, Toa Nuva of Ice, quietly. "There have been far too many secrets kept on this island."

The Toa Nuva filed away, heading in different directions. Only Takanuva remained behind with the Turaga of Fire.

"What troubles you, Toa?" asked Vakama. "Was my tale not what you expected?"

"It's not that," said Takanuva. "I have been a Matoran and now I am a Toa, and yet I still do not remember this city of Metru Nui! Why?"

"You will learn all, in time. Perhaps we should have shared all of this with you long ago, but we felt it would be cruel to remind you of a home you might never see again."

Takanuva nodded. "Perhaps that was wise, Turaga. But tell me, when you lived in Metru Nui — was it wonderful?"

"Wonderful . . . and terrible," said the Turaga. "I fear that when I have finished my tale, the Toa will have learned the true meaning of darkness."

BIONICLE®

Trial by Fire

For Heidi, my best friend
and a true joy to know

INTRODUCTION

Tahu Nuva, Toa of Fire, struggled to accept all that he had heard. Many a time he had listened to Turaga Vakama, elder of the village of Ta-Koro, tell a tale of past glories. But never such a story as this.

He had asked the Turaga to share with him and his fellow heroes a tale of Metru Nui. The Toa would soon be leading the Matoran villagers to this new island. They wished to be prepared for any danger that might await them there.

The tale Vakama told was a shocking one. He revealed that he and the other village elders had, long ago, been Matoran, living in a great city on Metru Nui. Through a strange twist of fate, they were gifted with the power of Toa. Their destiny: to save their city from disaster.

"We believed Metru Nui to be a paradise," Vakama had said. "But it was a city under siege. A dark, twisted plant called the Morbuzakh threatened from every side, bringing down buildings and driving Matoran from their homes. If left unchecked, nothing would remain of the city we loved."

But how to save the city? The answer came to Vakama in a vision. The Toa Metru had to seek out six Matoran who knew the hiding places of the Great Disks. These disks, when used together, could defeat the Morbuzakh. It seemed a simple task, and one that would surely prove to all in Metru Nui that these new Toa were worthy of being called heroes.

But the six Toa faced many dangers before the Matoran could be found. Still unskilled in the use of their powers, they barely escaped traps that had been set along their way. It soon became clear that one of the Matoran was seeking to betray the others, and all of Metru Nui as well.

It was at that point that Vakama had

stopped speaking. Now the Toa had gathered again to hear more of his strange tale.

Gali Nuva, Toa of Water, approached him quietly and laid a hand on his shoulder.

"Are you ready to continue, Turaga?" she asked. "Should we wait for another time?"

Vakama shook his head. "No, Toa Gali. These secrets have been kept from you for far too long. The time has come to speak. But . . . it is not easy."

"You said that you felt sure one of the six Matoran was walking in shadow," Tahu, Toa of Fire, said. "Why didn't you turn him over to the enforcers of order in Metru Nui — what did you call them?"

"Vahki," replied Vakama. "We had no choice. Those six Matoran were the only ones who knew the location of the Great Disks, and we had to have those disks. But we knew we must take precautions against betrayal."

"Tell us more, Turaga," said Pohatu. "Continue your story, please."

"Very well, Toa of Stone," said Vakama. "Now where was I? Oh, yes. With the six Matoran having been found, we Toa Metru were ready to begin searching for the Great Disks. Time was running out — with each day, the Morbuzakh grew bolder and more of the city was brought to ruin.

"It was decided that we would split into teams to search the city for the disks, bringing the Matoran with us. Of course, not everyone was happy about this idea. . . ."

"Next time, I'm picking the teams," grumbled Onewa, Toa Metru of Stone. He had been trudging along behind Vakama, Toa of Fire, and two of the Matoran for the better part of an hour. He hadn't bothered to keep his unhappiness a secret.

Nuhrii said nothing. A Matoran from the Ta-Metru district, all his energies were focused on finding the disks. In his mind, he saw himself showered with praise for helping to save the city and maybe even having a Mask of Power named after him someday. Turaga Dume, elder of Metru Nui, might even want a Matoran of such courage as an advisor.

The other Matoran on the journey, Ahkmou, was a Po-Matoran carver. He turned back to look at Onewa and said, "Since when did Onewa follow the rules? Has becoming a Toa

Metru made you soft? Leave these two fire-spitters behind and let's find the Great Disk ourselves."

"Sure," grunted Onewa. "And maybe walk into another trap. Don't think I've forgotten how hard it was to catch you, Ahkmou. I trust you about as far as I could throw the Great Temple."

Vakama was tempted to tell the bickering Po-Metru natives to be quiet, but that would probably just make things worse. Maybe it had been a mistake using Kanoka disks to choose the teams. But they were easy to find, since every Matoran used disks for sport, and the three-digit codes on them offered a simple way to decide. The two lowest codes worked together, the two highest, and so on. It was just bad luck he had wound up with Onewa. They just could not seem to get along.

They had crossed the border of Ta-Metru a short while ago. Nokama, Toa Metru of Water, had found a series of clues to the locations of the Great Disks carved on the wall of the Great Temple. According to the inscription, finding the

Ta-Metru disk required "embracing the root of fire." Vakama and Nuhrii both knew what that meant, but neither wanted to speak about it out loud.

Onewa and Ahkmou looked around, uncomfortably. Their home metru was known for its wide, flat expanses where massive sculptures were carved and stored. Ta-Metru, on the other hand, was a land of fire, where molten rivers of protodermis were forged into masks, tools, and other objects. Buildings crowded in close and all of them reflected the red glow of the furnaces. The sound of crafters' tools striking in unison and the hiss of cooling masks seemed to come from every side.

"I need a rest," said Ahkmou. "My feet are tired."

"Mine too," said Nuhrii. "Why couldn't we just take the transport chutes?"

Vakama frowned. He had insisted that they travel on foot, and Onewa had agreed. Taking the chutes would make it too easy for one or both Matoran to jump out midway and disappear into the streets and alleyways. "All right. But stay together and stay here."

The two Matoran sat down. Vakama walked away, expecting Onewa to keep an eye on them, but the Toa Metru of Stone followed him. "Do you know where we're going? What is this 'root of fire'?"

Vakama gestured toward the buildings that surrounded them. "Well, you know about the Great Furnace in Ta-Metru, and all the smaller furnaces and forges here. The flames that feed them come from fire pits . . . the 'roots' of the fire. They are highly dangerous places."

"Let me guess. Climbing down into one is against the law in Ta-Metru, so we're going to have Vahki squads to worry about."

"Probably."

"You had better be right about all this," Onewa said. "Or it's the last time I'm trusting you, fire-spitter."

Vakama felt anger rising in him, and this time didn't try to fight it off. "Do you have a better plan? These six disks are the only thing that can save Metru Nui. Unless we find them, the whole place is going to fall to the — Morbuzakh!"

The Toa Metru of Fire pointed over Onewa's shoulder, but his warning came too late. A twisted Morbuzakh vine snaked out of a chute and wrapped itself around Onewa, lifting the startled Toa into the air.

"My arms are pinned!" the Toa Metru of Stone shouted. "I can't get free!"

"Hang on! I'll save you!" Vakama said, thrusting a disk into his disk launcher.

"Hang on? Hang on to what??" The Morbuzakh was dragging Onewa toward the chute. Once inside, it would be too late to free him.

Vakama aimed carefully and launched his disk at the vine. When it struck, it sent bitter cold along the length of the plant, freezing it solid. With the pressure gone, Onewa was able to wriggle free. He hit the ground and looked from the vine to Vakama.

"Yeah, well," he muttered. "I could have done that myself . . . somehow." He idly swung his fist and shattered the frozen plant into a thousand icy shards.

Vakama turned and headed back toward where the Matoran waited. "You can have the next one then. Maybe if you grumble at it, it will go away."

"Hasn't worked with you," replied Onewa.

Vakama didn't answer. The spot where they had left Nuhrii and Ahkmou was empty. He felt a sinking feeling inside. If the two of them had vanished . . .

"There!" yelled Onewa. He pointed toward the two Matoran, who were fleeing in the direction of Po-Metru. The Toa of Stone whirled his proto-piton tool above his head and made a perfect throw, the cable wrapping around Ahkmou's legs. Smiling, Onewa began reeling in the Po-Matoran.

"Nice," said Vakama. "But here's an easier way." He took out a teleportation disk, checked its three-digit code to make sure it was low power, and then hurled it from his launcher. It struck Nuhrii a glancing blow and the Ta-Matoran disappeared. An instant later, he popped back into existence right in front of the two Toa.

"I guess you weren't that tired after all," said Vakama. "So let's keep moving."

"So have you ever visited these fire pits before?" Onewa asked.

"No," Vakama said softly. "Even mask makers are not allowed near them. The risk is too great."

"Scorched Matoran, right?"

"Not only that," said Vakama. "If anything happened to the flames in those pits, production in Ta-Metru would come to a halt." Seeing the lack of reaction on Onewa's face, he added, "There would be nothing for the Po-Matoran to carve."

They were working their way slowly toward the center of the city, trying to keep off the busier avenues. Onewa insisted the two Matoran stay close, while he himself kept scanning the alleys. Vakama did not need to ask why. They both could sense they were being followed.

At one point, just after they rounded a corner, Onewa gestured for them to flatten against the wall. They waited a long moment, but no one went by except the occasional Matoran. Finally, Onewa peered around the edge of the building and shook his head. "Not there."

"Who do you think it is?" asked Ahkmou.

"Guess," answered Onewa. A four-legged creature named Nidhiki had been chasing Ahkmou when Onewa found him. The same powerful being had been responsible for sabotage and traps encountered by the other Toa Metru in their search for the Matoran. Whoever he was, he did not want the Toa finding the Great Disks.

"Maybe we should get off the street," Vakama suggested. "We can take a shortcut through —"

"The protodermis reclamation furnace," Nuhrii finished. "The rear exit would bring us out near the fire pits."

"Lead the way," said Onewa. "All these fires, flames, and furnaces look alike to me."

* * *

The protodermis reclamation furnace was relatively small as Ta-Metru furnaces went, but its fires were just as hot and had plenty to burn. Damaged masks, tools and other items were sent here from the reclamation yard to be melted down. The resulting liquid protodermis was then fed through special channels back to the forges, where it could be used again. What went into the furnace was little more than garbage, but what came out might become something wonderful in the hands of a skilled crafter.

Its function made it ideal for use as a shortcut to the fire pits. For one thing, the place ran itself. Few, if any, Matoran actually worked there, so the building would most likely be empty. The Nuurakh, the Ta-Metru Vahki squads, did not bother patrolling in the area. After all, who would want to steal trash?

Vakama led the way as they slipped into the side entrance. The only light inside came from the fire in the furnace. The building consisted of a wide catwalk that ran along all four sides and looked down upon a long chute. The chute ran through the center of the building, carrying items directly from the yards to the flames. The air inside was heavy with smoke and the smell of melting protodermis.

Onewa walked to the edge of the catwalk and peered down. He had never seen anything like this. In his home district of Po-Metru, goods arrived already shaped, and carvers added the finishing touches. Watching masks and tools move slowly through a chute toward destruction was incredible, and even a little frightening.

Vakama joined him. "Sometimes I am not sure I like this place."

"Why not?"

"It keeps us from learning from our mistakes. We just melt them down and make them go away."

"Toa! Watch out!"

Neither Vakama nor Onewa had time to react to Nuhrii's shout. Twin blasts of energy struck them, sending them tumbling over the catwalk and through the energized walls of the chute. They hit hard and lay there, stunned, as the chute moved them closer and closer to the white-hot flames.

Nidhiki stepped out of the shadows. The two Matoran had run away, but there would be time to find them later. For now, he wanted to enjoy his victory over the two Toa Metru. He looked down at the unmoving forms of Vakama and Onewa, his dark laughter mingling with the crackling of the flames.

Nuju, Toa Metru of Ice, and Whenua, Toa Metru of Earth, moved slowly and quietly down a darkened corridor. All around them, eyes frozen in suspended animation seemed to watch their progress. The most fearsome creatures ever to appear in Metru Nui were preserved here in the Onu-Metru Archives, still-living exhibits to be studied by Matoran scholars.

Toa Nuju scowled as they walked through the latest in a series of seemingly endless hallways, filled with dusty display cases. Before he became a Toa, Nuju's job had been scanning the skies searching for hints of what the future held for Metru Nui. To him, the Archives were nothing but a monument to a dead past.

"I never knew this place was so big," he muttered.

"As big as it needs to be," replied Whenua,

with pride in his voice. "We've added two new sub-levels lately. The subterranean sections will someday stretch to the sea in every direction!"

"Why stop there? Why not just knock down the rest of the metru and turn the whole city into a dusty museum?"

Whenua glanced at Nuju with an expression of irritation. "That might be better than wasting time and space trying to predict tomorrows that might not come."

Nuju shook his head. They had been having some version of this argument since they left Ga-Metru on their search for the Great Disks. Neither one was going to change the other's mind, so there was no future in continuing. "Let's say we both live in the present for a moment. Do you think it was wise to leave Tehutti and Ehrye up above? What if they run off?"

"We left them in a section of the Archives that Tehutti had never visited before. Even the best Matoran archivist would get lost trying to find his way out of an unfamiliar wing, and he knows it. Oh, look at that! We found that insectoid arm digging sub-level 6. It's not Bohrok, but we're not sure what else it might have belonged to."

Nuju smiled. It was probably too much to ask to expect Whenua to stop giving tours. Even in the face of danger — the city threatened by the Morbuzakh plant, a handful of Matoran holding the key to its defeat — Whenua was still an old archivist at heart.

The carving at the Great Temple had advised that "no door must be left unopened" in Onu-Metru if the Great Disk were to be found. But the Archives contained hundreds of thousands of doors, if not more. Fortunately, Tehutti knew which level concealed the disk. Now the trick was finding it.

The two Toa Metru turned a corner. Before them, the hallway stretched as far as the eye could see. Each side was lined with doors easily four times the height of a Toa. The doors were thick and strong, too, and locked tight.

"Why all the locks?" Nuju asked. "Worried someone will break into the exhibits?"

Whenua chuckled. "No, Nuju. Worried that the exhibits will break *out.* Some of these creatures seem able to resist our efforts to put them in stasis."

The Toa Metru of Earth stopped at the first door on the left. No sign gave a hint of what lay behind it, but that wasn't unusual. One of the rules of the Archives was, "If you have to ask what's behind the door, you aren't meant to open it."

Nuju craned his neck to see the top of the massive door, then examined the equally oversized lock. "I don't suppose you have a key?"

"No. Only the Chief Archivist has keys to this level. If he knew we were rummaging around down here, the Vahki would already be on their way."

Nuju raised his crystal spike and fired a blast of ice at the lock, freezing it solid. "Then we make our own."

Whenua nodded and revved up one of his earthshock drills. It took only a brief touch to shatter the frozen lock.

The door slowly swung open. Nuju peered

inside. "Whenua? There is something in there. Much too big to be a Great Disk."

Before either of them could move, a gigantic Ussal crab claw shot from inside the room and clamped itself around the Toa. "Unngh! Wrong room! Wrong room!" Whenua shouted.

"I figured that out for myself," Nuju replied, straining against the mighty claw to no effect. He was secretly grateful that it was impossible to see the Ussal to which the claw belonged. This day had already had enough nasty surprises.

"This — owww! — is a very rare creature!" Whenua said. "Try not to hurt it!"

Nuju pitted every bit of his strength against the claw and didn't so much as loosen its grip. "We are rare creatures, too, Whenua. Right now, I would even say endangered!"

Whenua activated both of his earthshock drills, setting them spinning at a high rate of speed. "I think I have an idea, but it might bring the whole place down on us."

"Let me worry about the future," Nuju replied. "It's what I do best."

Whenua closed his eyes and concentrated on his Toa tools. The earthshock drills could bore through virutally any substance, even at low speed. But they had one other feature: when in use, they produced a loud hum.

If I can get them going fast enough, he thought. *Hit just the right frequency, maybe . . .*

The drills became a blur, whirling faster and faster. The hum went from painfully loud into the ultrasonic range. Whenua and Nuju both felt certain their heads would split open. Cracks began forming in the walls and ceiling. Whenua pushed as hard as he could to increase the speed, then pushed a little harder, doing his best not to scream from the strain.

Suddenly, they were free. Both Toa dropped to the ground as the monstrous claw retreated back into the darkness. Nuju slammed the door after it and created a new lock of thick ice. Then he turned to Whenua, who was slowly powering down his drills.

"Ow," said the Toa of Ice.

"Sorry. All that I could think of," Whenua

replied. "No one is quite sure what that thing is, possibly a hybrid of an Ussal crab and some larger creature. But we do know it's practically blind and uses its hearing to track prey."

"Sensitive ears," said Nuju. "You gave it a headache."

Whenua stood and helped Nuju to his feet. "Welcome to the Archives."

"We're lost-wandering," said Orkahm. The Le-Matoran looked fearfully around at the unfamiliar sights of Ga-Metru. "We're never going to find that Great Disk!"

Vhisola gave him a hard look. "We're not lost," the Ga-Matoran snapped. "Just a little . . . turned around."

"You said you knew where we were ground-walking."

"I do!" Vhisola insisted. "It's around here, somewhere."

"Enough," Nokama, Toa Metru of Water, said sternly. "Arguing won't get us to the Great Disk any faster. It might even make things worse, Vhisola," she added, pointing down the avenue.

The Ga-Matoran turned to look. Then she gasped and took a step backwards. Standing beside one of the canals up ahead were three other

Ga-Matoran, all of them watching the approaching group with suspicion. One of them whispered to another, who then ran off toward the Great Temple.

Matau, Toa Metru of Air, watched the Ga-Matoran disappear and said, "So? They are curious-watching. What is the worry?"

Nokama dropped her voice to a whisper. "It's more than that. Those Matoran have been claimed by the Bordakh, the Ga-Metru Vahki squad. One touch of a Bordakh staff and a Matoran becomes so dedicated to order that he will turn in his best friend to preserve it."

"Spies," Matau replied. "Then I have a thought-plan. If it works, then we meet at the spillway quick-soon. Understand?"

"Yes, but what — ?"

"Ha! What do you know about Great Disks?" Matau boomed loud enough for the whole street to hear. "I will track-find the disk before you three can even check one proto-dam." Then the Toa of Air swung up into a chute and was gone.

The two Matoran down the road seemed to think about it for a moment, then they dashed off in the direction Matau had gone. Once Nokama was sure they were well away, she started running, dragging Vhisola and Orkahm behind her.

"Hey! Stop it!" Vhisola cried.

"They will not be able find him, and once they realize that, they will come back here. We must be elsewhere."

The Toa Metru of Water led them on a winding path through alleys, behind schools, over walls and finally to the site of one of Ga-Metru's mini-dams. Here tides of protodermis were held back so as not to overflow the metru's canal system. Nokama scanned the area but saw no sign of any Vahki or watchful Matoran. But she did see Matau standing in the middle of the spillway, arms folded across his chest and smiling.

"What took you so long?" he laughed.

"You stay here," Nokama said to Vhisola and Orkahm. "Keep an eye out for Bordakh."

Before either could argue, she ran, jumped,

flipped in mid-air and landed beside Matau. They were standing in a wide stone channel through which liquid protodermis flowed into the canals as needed. Right now, it was bone dry and would stay that way as long as the main valve was closed.

"You lost them?" she asked.

"No one catches a Toa-hero," Matau answered, leaning in close. "Unless, of course, he wants to be caught."

"Provided anyone wants to catch him," Nokama replied. "If we let a little protodermis out, we can swim through some of the lesser canals right to the Great Temple. Vhisola says we will find the disk there."

"Swim?" Matau said, with obvious disgust. "A Toa of Air doesn't swim — he high-flies."

"If he wants to get spotted by the Vahki, he does, yes. Turn the valve, just a little, and get some protodermis running through here. I will get the Matoran."

Shrugging, Matau walked over to the large wheel that controlled the valve. Then he stopped.

"Nokama? This is already open-wide." He grabbed the wheel and tried to turn it, but it would not move. "And locked!"

"What?" Nokama shouted, rushing toward him. She could already hear the roar of a protodermis wave heading for the spillway. "Matau, get out of here! Get —"

The wave smashed into the Toa of Water, sending her tumbling end over end. An instant later, Matau, too, was swept up in the flood. Not having Nokama's experience as a swimmer, he had not thought to grab a breath. Now he floundered, hand to his throat as the liquid protodermis filled his mouth and lungs.

Nokama extended her hydro blades in front of her and knifed through the protodermis. She slammed into Matau, her momentum carrying them both up toward the lip of the spillway. Then they were out of the liquid, landing hard on the stone ledge.

She rolled the Toa of Air over. "Matau? Matau!" she cried.

Matau choked and gasped. Then his eyes

snapped open and he looked at Nokama, a smile spreading across his face. "I knew you cared."

Nokama, Matau, Vhisola, and Orkahm walked hurriedly toward the Great Temple. There was no way to reach it without being seen, but they did their best to stay inconspicuous. For two Toa Metru, it wasn't easy. Matoran looked at them with wonder and awe, sometimes even fear, but none seemed hostile.

"'In Ga-Metru, go beyond the depths of Toa before,'" said Nokama. "That's what the carving said."

"And what does that scratch-writing mean?" asked Matau.

"In the sea, below the Great Temple," answered Vhisola. "Far below."

"Oh. Happy-cheer," said Matau, not sounding happy at all.

They circled around behind the Great Temple. Only a narrow stone walkway separated the building from the sea. Nokama had already announced that she would be going down alone to retrieve the disk.

"You and Orkahm are not swimmers," she told Matau. "But if something goes wrong, if I don't return, you will need Vhisola to show you the way out. So she stays here."

Matau was going to argue that Toa-heroes should work together. But the memory of almost drowning in protodermis was enough to keep him quiet. "Go quick-fast then, Toa Nokama. We will be waiting."

Nokama nodded, then dove into the turbulent sea of protodermis and vanished beneath the waves. Toa and Matoran stared after her, wondering what she might be encountering far below.

So caught up were they that they never heard the approach of others until it was too late. Matau glanced to the left and saw to his surprise three Bordakh, staffs at the ready, closing in. Three more moved toward them from the right, leaving their only escape the cold sea.

"I hate Ga-Metru," he muttered.

* * *

Nokama was unaware of what was going on up above. She had reached the very foundation of the Great Temple and spotted her prize. Wedged between two jagged outcroppings up ahead was a Great Disk!

The sight gave her renewed energy. She dove deeper and used all her new Toa strength to pry the disk loose. She checked the three-digit code and confirmed that, yes, this disk had been made in Ga-Metru and had a power level of 9. Only Great Disks possessed so much raw energy.

Smiling, she tucked it under her arm and started for the surface. She never noticed that those two jagged outcroppings had been massive teeth, or that their owner objected to her intrusion. She kicked her legs and swam, even as a pair of massive jaws prepared to snap shut upon her.

The first thing Onewa felt was the heat. It was never this hot in Po-Metru, not even in a Sculpture Field in the middle of the day. What in the name of Mata Nui was going on?

That's when he opened his eyes and saw the flames leaping in the furnace. Suddenly, he remembered the blast, the fall, everything. He shook Vakama, saying, "Wake up! Might be your last chance!"

The Toa of Fire's eyes snapped open and he looked around. They had moved a long way through the chute and were almost in the mouth of the furnace. There was no time to jump out of the chute, and once inside the melting chamber, not even the power of the Toa would save them.

"Don't you have a disk for this?" asked Onewa.

"Quiet! I have to concentrate," Vakama answered. He reached out his hands toward the mouth of the furnace and struggled to call upon his Toa energies. He knew that he had the ability to create fire. Now he was gambling that he could control it as well.

The chute brought them closer and closer to the end. Onewa wondered if his Mask of Power might be able to rescue them, then sadly remembered that he did not even know what power his mask possessed. It was up to Vakama.

The Toa of Fire summoned every last bit of his willpower and hurled it at the furnace. Then, to his amazement, the fires began to flicker. He felt heat pouring into his body as the flames died down to mere sparks. Soon, even the sparks were gone.

"I don't believe it," Onewa whispered. "How did you — ?"

"Watch out!" Vakama yelled, just before unleashing twin white-hot bursts of flame that burned a hole through the ceiling of the building. The streams of fire lasted for a long, long moment before Vakama cut them off. Then he finally collapsed, exhausted.

"What did you do?"

"Absorbed the fire," said Vakama, out of breath. "But I couldn't contain the power. Had to release it, or . . ."

Onewa glanced up in time to see Nidhiki back away from the railing and vanish into the darkness. He considered giving chase, but he knew his four-legged enemy would already be long gone. Besides, there was a worse problem to be faced.

"That fire blast, Vakama, it's going to bring the Vahki on the run," he said, helping the Toa of Fire to his feet. "The Nuurakh will haul us in for destruction of metru property and our mission will be over."

"Nuhrii and Ahkmou?"

Onewa shook his head. "My guess is we're going to have to find them. Again. Let's go."

As it turned out, tracking down the two Matoran was not very difficult. Ahkmou had been to Ta-

Metru before, but didn't know it well, and wasn't willing to risk running into Nidhiki. Nuhrii did know all the alleyways and shortcuts, but was too frightened to go very far. Onewa found them hiding among some chutes that were closed for repair.

Vakama knelt down and looked at both of them. "Listen to me. It should be obvious now that someone doesn't want us to find the Great Disks. That means neither one of you is safe until they *are* found. Understand?"

Nuhrii nodded. Ahkmou shrugged. Vakama decided that would have to be enough.

"Then let's go to the fire pits."

The Ta-Metru fire pits consisted of a half dozen deep, narrow craters from which spewed forth great jets of flame. A nest of underground pipelines fed the fires to wherever they were needed in the metru. Given their importance, it was no surprise that the site was fenced in and guarded by Nuurakh.

"Can't we just go up and tell them why we need the disk?" asked Nuhrii.

"If they listened, and if they believed us, and if they were willing to take us to Turaga Dume to explain, maybe we would get the disk," said Onewa. "Or maybe not. So we bend the rules. Hey, you can't make a sculpture without shattering some protodermis, right?"

"We need a distraction," said Vakama.

Onewa smiled. "Done."

A few moments later, they were in position. Vakama and Nuhrii had crept as close to the fence as they could without being seen. Onewa and Ahkmou had moved near a pile of stone left over from a recent excavation.

At Vakama's signal, Onewa focused his elemental power. First, one block of stone went flying to crash against the fence. Then two, then six, until the Vahki rushed over to see what was happening. Onewa got a little carried away and sent a block crashing into one of the Nuurakh.

As soon as the Vahki had left their posts, Vakama and Nuhrii rushed forward. Vakama used his power to heat up the fence and melt a hole for the two of them. "Are you sure you know which fire pit contains the disk?" the Toa Metru whispered.

"I saw a carving," answered Nuhrii. "I think it was correct."

The Matoran led Vakama to the lip of one of the pits. The Toa of Fire peered over, then jumped back as the flames roared from it. Once the fires subsided, he said, "Come on, we don't have long!"

Melting handholds in the sides of the pit, Vakama climbed down with Nuhrii clinging to him. Down below, he could see a disk wedged into the wall, somehow intact despite the intense heat. Vakama reached down and pried it loose. Yes, it did have the symbol of Ta-Metru on it, and its three-digit disk code indicated it had a power level of 9 — the highest known concentration of energy possible in a Kanoka disk.

This was a Great Disk!

"We have it," said Vakama. "Climb over me and get out of the pit."

Nuhrii clambered over Vakama's shoulders, but before he could make it to the surface, twin Morbuzakh vines shot up from the depths below. They wrapped themselves tightly around Toa and Matoran and began to drag them down into the fire pit.

"Free yourself and get out of here! Get the Great Disk to Onewa!" Vakama shouted.

"I can't, it's too strong! We're Vahki bones!" Nuhrii answered, frantic. "The fire pit will erupt any moment!"

The Toa of Fire redoubled his efforts but the more he struggled, the harder the vine pulled. Worse, he was bound in such a way that there was no room in the pit for him to aim and launch a disk.

"Nuhrii, can you reach my last disk? I need you to load it in the launcher."

The Matoran nodded and strained to reach the disk. He could just barely brush his fingertips against it. "I can't reach!"

"Try! It's more than just us — the whole city is at stake," said Vakama.

Nuhrii stretched until the pain was so great he could barely think straight. But his hand closed around the disk. "It's a power level 4," he reported. "Power code I."

As Nuhrii fitted the disk in the launcher, Vakama continued to fight to get free. Power code I was able to reconstitute whatever it touched at random. It was a dangerous disk to use because it was just as apt to make the Morbuzakh more powerful than less. But they had no choice.

Nuhrii wrestled against the might of the Morbuzakh to get the launcher into the right position. When it was as well-aimed as he could manage, he triggered the mechanism and launched the disk at the spot where the two vines joined.

It struck the target head-on. Vakama watched, amazed, as the molecules that made up the vines were scrambled. The shock made the plant loosen its grip. The Toa of Fire and Nuhrii scrambled out of the pit.

Vakama caught a flash of the new form of the Morbuzakh — a thick vine with long, sharp thorns and what looked like a mouth lined with razor-sharp teeth. It gave out an eerie howl and tried to reach Vakama, just as the pit exploded into flames again. The Toa Metru knew the flames would not destroy the vine, but he had no wish to wait around and see that horror again.

Toa and Matoran ran for the fence. Both made a point of not looking behind them.

"What about this one?" asked Nuju, pointing to a metallic door that looked thick and solid.

Whenua turned, looked, and shook his head. "No. It's not behind that one."

"How do you know?"

"Because I know what's in there. Leave it alone."

Nuju glared at the Toa of Earth. Back in Ko-Metru, Nuju had been an important scholar with vital responsibilities. Now he was a Toa Metru, reduced to tramping around dark, musty Archives looking for one relic among thousands. So far, he had been squeezed in an Ussal crab claw, weakened by a frost leech, stepped in something whose origin he really did not want to know, and gotten hopelessly lost at least twice. He was covered in the dust of the past and he did not like it.

"Whenua doesn't seem to have any idea

what is down here," Nuju muttered to himself. "So how does he know the Great Disk isn't behind this door?"

Checking to make sure the Toa of Earth was otherwise occupied, Nuju grasped the handle of the door and pulled. Surprisingly, it wasn't locked. It took his eyes a moment to adjust to the even deeper darkness behind the door. Once they had, he noticed something that seemed to be shimmering. Could the Great Disk create an effect like that?

He took a step inside, then another, before his progress was stopped by a clear wall. No, it wasn't a wall. It was the side of a tank filled with liquid protodermis. He pressed his mask against the glass, trying to see what, if anything, was in there.

Suddenly something slammed hard against the inside of the tank, right where Nuju was standing. Before the Toa could react, it had circled and smashed into the tank wall again, this time creating a hairline crack. On its third pass, Nuju got a good look at it, and wished he hadn't.

The creature was long, serpent-like, with powerful forearms and, most disturbing, two heads. Both heads featured narrow greenish eyes and a fanged mouth.

Nuju jumped back as it struck again. Now protodermis was starting to leak from the tank, but this was something he could handle. A minimal amount of his power was enough to freeze it and seal the crack. But his presence had obviously disturbed the creature, so he felt that he had better leave.

He turned around. Whenua was standing in the doorway, watching him.

"Done?" asked the Toa of Earth. "Listen, I know you don't like it here. It's not neat and orderly like Ko-Metru. Archivists don't sit in clean towers studying all day, they are out getting their hands dirty. But we have rules here too — like don't annoy the two-headed Tarakava, if at all possible."

Nuju nodded. "It does seem . . . excitable."

"Last ones to excite it before it came here were two Ga-Matoran in a fishing skiff," Whenua said, turning and walking away. "They were lucky to make it out of the sea. The skiff wound up as sawdust."

Nuju said nothing. He followed behind Whenua, reminding himself that even in a place devoted to the dead past, actions could have consequences.

Whenua stopped at another doorway. His expression was troubled. "It could be in here. It probably would be in here, the way things are going. But, by Mata Nui, I hope it's not."

This door actually had a sign, which read "Keep out." Nuju wondered what could be behind there that would worry Whenua so much. After all, two Toa Metru should be able to handle anything.

Whenua hesitated before using his earthshock drill to punch through the lock. "I hope we're ready for this. The last archivist that came down here hasn't spoken a word since. Screams a lot, though."

Nuju readied both of his crystal spikes, in case his ice power would be needed. Whenua slowly opened the door and the two of them stepped inside.

They found themselves in a large, brightly lit room. It was completely bare. There was no sign that any creature lived there, or ever had lived there. Nuju frowned. *This didn't look very frightening at all. What had Whenua been so worried about?*

Both Toa Metru whirled at the sound of the door slamming behind them. Even more surprising, Nuju could see the hole made by Whenua's drills disappearing. They were locked in.

"What is this?" asked Nuju.

"No one knows exactly," said Whenua, looking all around. "Our best theory is that this creature has some connection to the random reconstitution disk power."

"*What* creature? There's nothing here!" said Nuju.

"You don't understand," Whenua replied, as the lightstones suddenly began to dim. "This Rahi isn't in the room. It *is* the room!"

The floor beneath Nuju's feet began to

shift. A pair of clawed hands emerged from the stone to grasp him around the ankles. A much larger hand sprang forth from one of the walls and narrowly missed grabbing Whenua. The room echoed with a low, ominous rumble that sounded like the breathing of a massive creature.

The Toa of Earth dove toward where Nuju stood. Spikes shot out of the walls just above him, but Whenua was too nimble to be caught. He grabbed the two hands holding Nuju and wrenched them free. The roar in the room grew louder and angrier.

Now the floor was rising fast, sending both Toa toward a crushing end against the ceiling. Nuju fired streams of ice from his crystal spikes, forming thick pillars to keep floor and ceiling apart. But he knew they would not hold for long.

"We have to get out of here," he said.

"Any ideas?" asked Whenua.

"I was hoping you had one."

Whenua smiled. "Maybe I do. You can do ice, but what else can you do?"

Nuju needed no more prompting. He gathered his energies and concentrated on conjuring a storm. It was incredibly hard, unskilled as he still was in the use of his elemental powers. But little by little the air began to turn colder, and a chill wind started to blow through the confines of the room. Moisture in the air condensed into droplets, which then froze into crystals of snow.

Nuju strained to lower the temperature more, and then still more. Beside him, Whenua shivered, frost forming on his mask. It was an open question who would succumb to the storm first, the Toa Metru or the creature that had trapped them.

Then Whenua was pointing to something on the far wall. Nuju strained to see through the snow and ice. It looked like an opening in the wall. As the two Toa moved toward it, a wave passed through the floor beneath them, hurling them toward the gap. They flew out of the room and crashed against the wall of the hallway. Behind them, the gap closed again.

Whenua groaned and brushed the ice off his body. "I guess it worked. This hasn't been as easy as I thought it would be."

"Maybe that's the first lesson in the life of a Toa," replied Nuju. "Nothing is easy."

The Toa of Ice was starting to feel he was walking in circles. This sub-level of the Archives seemed to go on forever, and he felt certain they had seen some of these doors before. But Whenua insisted that wasn't so.

"If it's here, we will have to find it soon," the Toa of Earth insisted. "We have explored almost the entire level. I don't think —"

He stopped abruptly and cocked his head, listening to something. Now Nuju could hear it too — the steady tramp of feet from somewhere in the halls. The footsteps were too heavy to be Matoran, and anyway archivists avoided this section.

Whenua glanced at Nuju. "We just ran out of time. The Vahki are coming. Someone must have heard all the noise down here and called for them."

The Toa of Earth started frantically opening doors. "We're down here without authorization, planning to take an artifact. Never mind that it's in a good cause. You know the Onu-Metru Vahki. The Rorzakh will chase us through this entire place and all the way back to the Great Temple before they give up!"

Nuju had to admit he was right. Even in Ko-Metru, Matoran knew never to get a Rorzakh on their trail. There was no risk they wouldn't take to get their job done. There was even a story that a Rorzakh had once plunged into a mine shaft, in free fall, to try and catch a lawbreaker.

The Toa of Ice started pulling open doors on the run. "I never imagined being a Toa would involve searching for so many things. I thought Toa had everything they needed."

"Maybe not," said Whenua. "Maybe Toa are just the only ones who have the power to find what has to be found."

The Toa of Earth yanked another door open. An avalanche of Metru Nui artifacts tumbled out, knocking him off his feet and burying him beneath a pile of tools, masks, stone tablets, and more.

For a moment, all was silent. Nuju took a step toward the pile when the artifacts started to shift. Then Whenua's hand shot out of the pile, holding the Great Disk.

Nuju smiled. It was time to gather the two Matoran and head to Ko-Metru where, he was certain, the search for the Great Disk would proceed in a much more orderly way.

Nokama swam in long, steady strokes, her eyes focused on the surface. She could make out indistinct figures through the water. There was Matau, and Vhisola, Orkahm, and . . . Vahki!

The sight made her stop short. Only then did she sense the disturbance in the water, as if nature itself were crying out to her. She whirled to see the giant sea beast closing in on her. She wanted to scream, but opening her mouth underwater would save the Rahi the trouble of ending her existence.

Nokama forced her fear away. It was all right for a Matoran to be afraid, but she was a Toa now. She could fight back, and just maybe solve two problems at once.

Clutching the Great Disk tightly, she sped for the surface. The monstrous Rahi was right on top of her, caught up in the hunt and determined to catch a meal. Nokama burst out of the water and into the air, diving toward one group of Vahki. The beast followed close behind, leaping, jaws snapping, hungry for its prey.

At the last possible moment, Nokama curled into a ball and flipped downwards. Unable to change direction, the Rahi slammed into the startled Vahki. Matau used the distraction to summon a strong wind and blow the other Vahki into the water.

"Now we are in trouble-danger," said Matau. "Vahki hate fish. And baths."

"Then let's not wait for their complaints," said Nokama. "We have the disk. Let's go!"

The four did not stop running until they had reached the borders of Le-Metru. Here they lost themselves in the crowds that filled the transport hub of Metru Nui. Vhisola kept looking over her shoulder as if she expected the Vahki to be gaining.

"Why am I here?" she asked. "You have the

Ga-Metru disk. I don't know anything about the Le-Metru disk! Why can't I go home?"

"You are safer with us," said Nokama.

"Yes, four-legged Rahi-breath out there somewhere," added Matau. "You wouldn't want to run into him."

Neither Toa Metru chose to tell the whole story. Each of the six Matoran who had joined the Toa on their quest for the disks had their own reasons for wanting the artifacts. For some, it was personal glory, for some spite, and the heroes believed Ahkmou wanted the disks for far darker reasons. Both Nokama and Matau felt letting either of their Matoran wander off was risking more trouble with the Vahki, or worse.

Matau led them to a strangely quiet section of the metru, marked by broken chutes and mangled support beams. No repair crews were in sight, nor any chute operators. Nokama glanced at Matau, who said simply, "Morbuzakh."

The Toa of Water looked around, concerned. An area of the metru ravaged by Morbuzakh vines would make a good hiding place, but it also meant the plant might strike here again. They would have to be on their guard.

"What did the carving-speak say about the Le-Metru disk?" Matau asked.

"The Great Disk of Le-Metru will be all around you when you find it," answered Nokama.

Matau looked left and right. "I don't see it."

"That's because it's not here," said Orkahm. "You won't find it by moving fast, Matau. As hard as it might be for you, you will have to slow down to retrieve it."

Matau frowned. To a high-flying Toa Metru like him, "slow down" sounded like a curse. "So where is it hidden-lost?"

"That's just it," said Orkahm. "I found it, but it's not in that place anymore. It could be anywhere by now. It's in a force sphere!"

Matau sat down heavily, his eyes on the ground. Nokama looked from him to Orkahm and back again. "Is that bad?" she asked.

"Very," Matau replied, nodding. "Very, very."

"Is someone going to explain to me what's going on, or do you need a downpour to convince you?" she snapped.

"All right, you know what a chute is?" said Orkahm. "It's protodermis with a magnetic energy sheath that keeps things fast-moving through it. Sometimes, if there's a break-flaw in the chute construction, some of that energy snaps off and wraps-folds in on itself."

"It travels everquick through the chutes," said Matau. "Its magnetism draws things inside: tools, debris . . . and a Great Disk. The longer it exists, the more mighty-strong it becomes."

"And then what happens?" asked Nokama, not sure she wanted to hear the answer.

"When it gets big enough and strong enough, it rips-tears chutes to pieces," said the Toa of Air. "Force sphere gets deep-buried under the wreckage and implodes. All gone."

"Along with everything inside it," said Nokama grimly. "We have to find it!"

Orkahm pulled out a chute map of Le-

Metru and showed it to the two Toa, pointing to one junction close by. "It was here just before Toa Matau and I high-flew to the Great Temple."

Toa Matau traced the force sphere's most likely route until he came to a spot on the map that looked to Nokama like a complete tangle of chutes. "There! Too many chutes wrapped around each other will slow it down. We'll find it there!"

"There" turned out to be an ancient portion of the metru, apparently built long before anyone tried making sense of the chute system. Nokama had never seen anything quite so complex or scrambled together. She wondered how any Matoran made it through what Matau called "the Notch."

The Toa of Air was perched up above one of the chutes, his keen eyes scanning the route. If he was right, the force sphere would come flying by any moment. All he would have to do would be jump inside it, grab the Great Disk, and then get back out.

"Easy!" he insisted. "Except for the getting

out. And the getting in. And maybe seek-finding the disk."

Orkahm cried out. The force sphere was barreling through the chute, heading for the Notch at an incredible rate of speed. It was larger than a Toa and its interior was a whirlpool of magnetic energy and protodermis fragments. Nokama questioned whether anything living could survive in there.

If Matau was worried, he didn't show it. As the sphere passed through the chute beneath him, he dove inside.

Instantly, the energies of the sphere took hold of him, threatening to tear him to pieces. Tools, bolts, and other small items swirled about him in a mad dance, striking him again and again. Meanwhile, the sphere continued on its rapid pace toward the Notch.

Outside, Orkahm's eyes widened. He and Matau had been wrong. The sphere was not going to slow down for the Notch! It was going to rip it to pieces and then collapse in on itself, taking the Toa of Air and the Great Disk with it.

Matau could sense what was happening, but it was too late to do anything about it. If he jumped out now, he would lose the Great Disk and the city would be doomed. If he stayed, at least there was a slim chance he could —

Yes! Reaching out blindly, he had grasped something that felt like a disk. Fighting the pull of the sphere, he brought it close enough to his mask to see it was indeed the Le-Metru Great Disk. As he admired it, a chunk of protodermis smashed into his hand, almost making him lose his grip.

Matau couldn't see out of the sphere, but he knew the Notch had to be coming up fast. He had to overcome the sphere's pull and leap out now, but there was nothing to brace himself against. Without that, he could do nothing but tumble helplessly like all the rest of the sphere's captive debris.

My own strength will not be enough, he told himself. *I will have to match my Toa-power against it.*

The last time Matau had used his elemental abilities, it had taken all his concentration to form just a simple cushion of air. This time, it seemed to come a little easier, but he was also attempting a much harder task. It was going to take a mini-cyclone to overcome the force sphere's power and tear himself free.

There was no time to let the winds build up slowly. Matau pushed his powers to their limit, forcing the air around him to swirl violently. Suddenly, he was in the center of a whirlwind which sucked the breath from his lungs. It was an open question whether the implosion would end his existence or suffocation would do it first.

The world became a blur as Matau spun around and around inside the cyclone. He could feel himself beginning to black out, but knew if he did, the windstorm would cease and any hope of escaping the sphere would be gone. He fought to stay conscious. After all, it wouldn't look very impressive to Nokama if the Toa of Air perished on his first big mission.

Then suddenly he was flying through the air. It took him an instant to realize he had been thrown free of the force sphere. Unfortunately, his whirlwind was still active, sending him hurling into a support post with a loud crash.

Nokama, Vhisola, and Orkahm ran over to where Matau lay on the ground. The Toa of Air wasn't moving. Hesitantly, Nokama reached out and touched his shoulder. "Matau?"

He rolled over abruptly and, smiling, thrust up a hand holding the Great Disk. "See, Nokama?" he said. "I told you, no worry-problem!"

In Metru Nui, Ko-Matoran were known for many things. Their devotion to learning was second to none. Their ambition to become Knowledge Tower scholars was incredibly powerful. Their attitude toward Matoran from other metru was usually cold, and sometimes bordered on rude. Since they almost always had their attention focused on a tablet, a carving, or some complicated philosophical problem, they often missed things going on around them.

That was why none of the Ko-Matoran bothered to look up and notice Toa Metru Whenua hanging on to a tower for dear life.

"I thought you were good at this," Nuju snapped, scrambling to pull his fellow Toa back onto the roof.

"No, that's Onewa who swings around

buildings," shouted Whenua. "I'm Whenua, who falls off them!"

With a mighty heave, Nuju succeeded in yanking the Toa of Earth back to relative safety on top of the ice-covered Knowledge Tower. Whenua immediately used his earthshock drills to dig himself handholds.

"Don't damage the crystal underneath," warned Nuju. "I should have gone with my first instinct and done this by myself. I knew what the consequences of this alliance would be."

"We worked together all right in Onu-Metru. Remember? Oh, I forgot, you ignore the past, don't you?" Whenua replied. "Besides, if you worked alone, you would probably just wind up like poor Tehutti."

The Onu-Matoran was standing on a nearby rooftop with Ehrye, his eyes wide and confused. Ehrye had a grip on his arm to keep him from wandering off. The four of them had encountered a patrol of Keerakh, the Ko-Metru Vahki, and Tehutti had made the mistake of running. One swipe of a Keerakh staff and he lost all sense of time and place. Judging by the things he had said since, Tehutti thought he was back in the Archives cataloging a Fikou spider exhibit.

"Are you sure the Great Disk is up here?" Whenua asked, getting cautiously to his feet. The winds were strong this high up and the Knowledge Tower rooftops had steep inclines. One slip and down he would tumble again.

"You were there when Nokama translated the carving," replied Nuju. "In Ko-Metru, find where the sky and ice are joined. Besides, Ehrye says it is near here, atop one of these Knowledge Towers."

Nuju stood at the edge of the roof and studied the gap between this tower and the next. His first attempt to travel by ice slide had failed miserably, so he was reluctant to do it again. Better to leap and rely on his crystal spikes to stop any fall.

Taking a running start, Nuju jumped into space. He had gauged his leap perfectly, arcing down close enough to the next tower that he could catch the side with a spike and anchor himself. Back on the other roof, Whenua looked on, frustrated.

Nuju raised his free spike and fired a blast of ice. When he was done, there was a thick, frozen beam in place between the two towers. "Wrap your arms around it and slide across," he instructed Whenua.

The Toa of Earth did some quick calculations, which included his new mass post-transformation, the thickness of the ice, and the velocity he would achieve just before he was smashed flat on the ground below. When he was done, he reported, "It will never hold."

"Yes, it will," Nuju insisted. "Probably," he added quietly.

Whenua jumped, caught the ice beam, and rapidly slid across the gap. He had made it halfway when the ice began to crack and splinter behind him. He struck the side of the building and dug in his earthshock drills even as the beam collapsed completely.

"Ko-Metru needs more chutes," Whenua muttered.

"Most Ko-Matoran don't travel by rooftop," said Nuju. "Look below."

Looking down was not high on Whenua's list of things to do, but the urgency in Nuju's voice left no room for argument. The Ko-Matoran far below looked like microscopic organisms, but those weren't what Nuju was pointing out. No, it was the half dozen Keerakh scuttling through the crowd and heading right for this particular Knowledge Tower that had the Toa of Ice worried.

"I thought we had left them far behind," said Whenua.

"Keerakh are efficient," answered Nuju. "We are not where we're supposed to be. It's their job to change that. Keep moving."

The two Toa Metru made it to the top of the tower. Whenua looked over the side and saw the Keerakh were climbing up the side of the building. "We have problems, Nuju."

"Worse than you know," said Nuju, pointing to the next tower. Three more of the Ko-Metru Vahki were gathered on its roof, waiting.

"Keerakh have found a way to take the element of chance out of tracking. They simply figure out where you are going and get there first."

"Have a plan?"

"Something like that," said Nuju, levelling his crystal spike and sending a blast of ice at Whenua. Instantly, the Toa of Earth was covered in a thick layer of ice from shoulders to knees.

"What are you doing?" Whenua demanded, struggling in vain to get free.

Nuju ignored him and turned to the Vahki on the opposite roof. "After a long pursuit, I have caught this thief from Onu-Metru. Take him to Turaga Dume for punishment."

The three Vahki looked at each other, obviously trying to figure out when the strange being with the twin spikes joined their side. With the closest thing Keerakh could give to a shrug, they sprang from their perch to take custody of Whenua.

In mid-leap, Nuju caught them with an ice blast and froze them solid. One swipe of his spike shattered the ice surrounding Whenua. "The

Vahki have kindly provided us with a bridge. Let's use it."

The two Toa Metru ran across the bridge of frozen Keerakh to the next roof. Nuju looked over his shoulder to make sure Ehrye and Tehutti were well-hidden a few towers back, then turned his attention to Whenua. "Are you all right?"

"Well, I won't be in a hurry to visit the icier parts of the Archives for a while," the Toa of Earth replied. "Next time, give me a little warning."

"All right. Hit the ground," said Nuju as he dove flat on the roof. Whenua joined him just as Nuju used his spikes to create a thin layer of snow and ice over them both. "Keep quiet," the Toa of Ice whispered.

Whenua could barely make out what was going on outside their icy shell. He spotted the shapes of the Keerakh reaching the top of the other roof. Half of them immediately went to work chipping away at the ice bridge while the other half crossed it in pursuit. One walked right over where the Toa lay, camouflaged.

Whenua started to rise. Nuju grabbed his arm and said softly, "Not yet. Wait."

"Wait? Wait for what?"

"You're the archivist," Nuju said quietly. "What do you know about Keerakh?"

"Let's see. Ko-Metru Vahki. Order enforcement technique is disorientation. Hard to hide from because they're always one . . . step . . . ahead of . . ." Whenua smiled.

"Exactly," said Nuju. "I do not know how they do it, but they do. So rather than run from them —"

"We follow them," Whenua finished. "And they lead us right to the Great Disk."

Of course, following Vahki was easier said than done. In their dormant state, Vahki occupied a circular hive, with one Vahki monitoring each direction. Though they appeared to be completely inactive, Vahki sensory apparatus never fully shut down. Any sound or movement was instantly detected. When Vahki traveled, they moved in much the same way, always with an eye turned toward the flanks and rear.

For that reason, Nuju had recommended that Ehrye and Tehutti be left behind. Tehutti kept ranting about misfiled Fikou anyway, and Ehrye was in no hurry to walk into a possible Keerakh trap. So the two Toa Metru traveled alone, relying on speed and stealth to keep up with the Vahki and keep out of sight.

Their journey ended at a central tower. The half dozen Vahki paused there and began to mill around. After a few moments, each Keerakh locked its four legs into place on the icy roof and settled in to wait.

Nuju frowned. "Of course, there is one problem with this plan."

"That's a change — you not thinking ahead," said Whenua. "Maybe what the Vahki need is a little disorder. Get me down from up here."

Nuju moved to the far edge of the rooftop and checked to make sure the Vahki had not yet noticed their presence. Then he used his elemental energies to create a thick pole of ice stretching from the roof to the avenue below.

"I was thinking more like pointing me toward a chute," said Whenua.

"This is faster."

"Right. At least it will be over quick," said Whenua, getting ready to ride down the pole. "When you see your opportunity, get that disk. I'll meet you in Ga-Metru."

Nuju watched as the Toa of Earth slid down and vanished in the icy mist. Then he went back to watching the Vahki.

Down below, Whenua was doing his best not to get sick. He was moving much too fast, with no way to slow down. At this rate, he would succeed in distracting the Vahki by making a very large hole in the street.

On the rooftop above, Nuju was counting quietly to himself. When he reached 10, he launched two more bursts of ice from his crystal spikes. They arced over the side of the building and disappeared.

Whenua saw the ice bolts approach and then pass him. The next thing he knew, he was flying down a winding ice slide that had suddenly formed around the pole. The angle of the slide kept changing so that, little by little, Whenua's descent was slowed. He still hit the ground hard, but Nuju's calculations were correct. The Toa of Earth hadn't suffered any serious injury.

That's the second time he's surprised me today, thought Whenua. *Hope it isn't going to become a habit.*

He looked around. A few Ko-Matoran had looked up from their studies long enough to notice that a Toa Metru had just dropped into their midst. It was only a matter of time before one summoned additional Vahki. Whenua went to work, using his earthshock drills to cut a hole in the street.

Once the opening was wide enough, the

Toa dropped down. As an archivist, he knew the underground of Metru Nui better than any of the other Toa. Immediately beneath the streets were mechanisms designed to help keep the metru clean, protodermis pipes, and the occasional nest of rodent Rahi. Farther down would be whatever sub-levels of the Archives had extended this far, and beneath that . . . beneath that, he preferred not to think about.

For now, he was only worried about the immediate sub-surface. Using one drill to bore through the street above, he used the other to disrupt the cleaning mechanisms, break the occasional narrow pipe, and generally make a mess. He made no effort to keep it quiet — the more noise the better.

He knew what would be happening above right now. Ko-Matoran would be looking around in wonder and annoyance at the disturbance. The sound would be traveling up to the sensitive ears of the Vahki. They would never be able to resist the chance to clamp down on such obvious disorder.

* * *

High above, the Vahki were proving Whenua right. First one, then two, peered over the side of the roof to see what was happening below. Unable to get a good look due to the icy mist that perpetually hovered over Ko-Metru, the Vahki squad left their positions and began climbing down the side of the Knowledge Tower.

Nuju waited until they were gone, then leapt to the next roof. He was sure the Great Disk must be there somewhere, but he saw no sign of it. He scrambled to get a little higher on the inclined roof and slipped, hurtling toward the edge.

Before he could put his crystal spikes to use, he had fallen over the side. At the last moment, he reached out and grabbed a huge icicle that hung from the ledge. It wasn't unusual to see icicles up this high, but he quickly noticed that this one was just a little different from the rest.

Frozen in its heart was a Great Disk.

Beneath the street, Whenua continued his labors, keeping an eye on the hole through which he had come. As soon as he saw Keerakh peering down through it, he knew it was time to be elsewhere. Revving up his drills, he punched a hole through the floor and then through the next level as well. Plunging through the gap, he tumbled into an Archives sub-level.

No Ko-Metru Vahki would ever find him down here. He took off at a run, following the winding corridors in the direction of Ga-Metru. If all had gone well, he would meet Nuju there with two Great Disks between them.

Toa Onewa and Ahkmou walked side by side through the Po-Metru sculpture fields, Vakama and Nurhii bringing up the rear. The journey had been made largely in silence, with the exception of Ahkmou giving directions to the hiding place of the Great Disk. They had already taken a few wrong turns thanks to the Matoran's "forgetting" exactly where it was concealed.

"It's not far," Ahkmou said.

"That's the tenth time you've said that," Onewa replied. "I'm beginning to think you don't want us to find the Great Disk."

"Of course I do," said Ahkmou. "Okay, so maybe I wanted them for myself at first. But now I realize that you six Toa need them to save the whole city. I wouldn't get in the way of that. Only, what are you going to do with the Great Disks once you have them?"

Onewa shrugged. "I don't know. This is Vakama's plan. I suppose we'll give them to him."

Ahkmou chuckled. "I see. So he gets all of you to go out and gather the six most powerful items in all of Metru Nui, and then you just turn them over to him? No questions asked? I wish I had thought of that."

I bet you do, thought Onewa darkly.

"So who's this four-legged friend of yours? The one who likes pushing Toa into furnaces?" asked the Toa of Stone.

"He's no friend," answered Ahkmou. "We were . . . business partners. He asked me to get him the Great Disks. Doing it seemed like a better idea than having him angry at me. He didn't say why he wanted them."

"And you didn't ask. What did he promise you in return?"

"Protection," said Ahkmou. "Something we both need right now. Look!"

Po-Matoran were running from the Sculpture Fields in a panic. Only two things had been known to make crafters move that fast: quitting time and a rogue tunneler. Unfortunately, it was too early for work to be done for the day.

Tunnelers had been a problem in Po-Metru for as long as Onewa could remember. They were lizard-like Rahi, normally about twice as long as Matoran were tall, with an appetite for solid protodermis. They had been known to dig up into warehouses and consume everything from raw protodermis blocks to finished tools. Rarely did they pose a real threat to the Matoran workers, but every now and then one went bad and began rampaging through the work areas.

Vakama and Nuhrii had caught up now. "What's going on?" asked the Toa of Fire.

"A little problem," said Onewa.

"A big problem," corrected Ahkmou.

The tunneler had emerged from beneath the surface into the middle of the Sculpture Field. It was bigger than any Onewa had ever seen, easily three times the size of a Toa. Worse, its scales were mottled with dark patches and its eyes were red. In a tunneler, both were sure signs of madness.

"Maybe I can scare it off," suggested Vakama. Before Onewa could stop him, he had lobbed a few small fireballs in the direction of the tunneler. Not wanting to hurt the beast, Vakama had aimed well over its head.

If the tunneler could have smiled, it would have. As the fireballs approached, it reared up on its hind legs and purposely let itself be hit. An instant later, it had transformed from a creature of scales and claws to a monster of flame.

"We're not in your metru, Vakama. Fire's not the answer to everything," Onewa said sharply. "Tunnelers absorb whatever power you throw at them. We've gone from a menace to a catastrophe."

All around the creature, sculptures had begun to melt. Every step it took left a charred footprint in the soil. Even at a great distance, the two Toa Metru could feel the heat.

"If that thing makes it out of the Sculpture Fields, all of Po-Metru could burn," said Onewa. "Let's see if it wants to play catch."

The Toa of Stone lifted a huge boulder and prepared to throw it. Vakama couldn't understand his strategy — most of the rock would melt before it ever reached the tunneler, and what was left wouldn't do any damage.

Onewa tossed the boulder. It began to glow and melt as it got closer to its target. But enough made it through that the tunneler had to bat the fragments away with its tail. As soon as rock met tunneler, the creature transformed again, this time becoming a thing of stone.

"Well, that helps a little," said Onewa. The tunneler brushed lightly against a massive sculpture, and the statue crumbled from the blow. "Or not."

"I have an idea, but we'll need Nuhrii and Ahkmou's help," said Vakama. He turned around and saw both Matoran were gone. A moment later, he heard the sounds of a struggle from behind one of the sculptures.

The Toa of Fire looked behind the statue. Nuhrii had Ahkmou pinned on the ground.

"He was trying to run away again," said the Ta-Matoran. "But he brought us here. Seems to me he should help us get out again."

"You're both going to help. Here's what we're going to do."

The tunneler slowly blinked its stone eyes. Two of the little ones were still in its sight, jumping and yelling in a language it didn't understand. The two larger ones had disappeared. Ordinarily, there was no cause to harm little ones, unless they got in the way of a meal. But these two were annoying with their noise.

With a snarl, the tunneler lumbered forward to silence them.

"Now!" shouted Onewa. He slung his proto piton onto a nearby statue and he and Vakama swung from their perch high above. As they passed over the tunneler, Vakama unleashed a quick, intense fire blast at the ground.

Fire met sand right in front of the creature,

fusing the ground into glass. Startled by the light and heat, the creature whipped its tail forward, striking the new glass surface. That was all it took for the tunneler of stone to change to a tunneler of crystal.

The creature spotted the two Toa Metru and started to take a step forward, only to be stopped by the sound of a sharp crack. Its new glass body wasn't strong enough to support the tunneler's size. Every move it made caused another hairline fracture to appear, so the tunneler wisely decided to stay still.

"That should keep it occupied until the Vahki arrive," said Onewa. "Then the archivists can decide what to do with it."

Onewa looked up at the tallest sculpture he had ever seen. It looked like an upside down mountain, balancing on its peak. Nokama had said that the Toa must seek a "mountain in balance" if they were to find the Po-Metru Great Disk. This certainly looked like the spot.

"It's up there," confirmed Ahkmou. "Embedded in a jagged hole near the top. Good luck getting it out."

The thought of the climb made even the Toa of Stone a little dizzy. He had no doubt he could get up there. It was getting down that might pose a problem.

"Are you sure you want to go up there alone?" asked Vakama. "I could —"

"No," Onewa replied. "If I have to be concerned about me falling, I don't want to have to be worrying about you falling too. Besides, if I don't make it down . . ."

Vakama nodded. Risking both Toa Metru would be foolish. Someone had to be left to get the Great Disk if Onewa failed.

The Toa of Stone dug one of his proto pitons into the side of the sculpture and began to climb. Vakama, Ahkmou, and Nuhrii watched him as he slowly ascended, each alone with his thoughts.

Onewa moved slowly, but steadily. His new body was far stronger than his Matoran form had been, but still his shoulders and arms already ached from the effort. And there was still so far to go.

His thoughts drifted back to the Great Temple and the moment he and the others had become Toa. He had certainly never imagined, when he brought the Toa stone there, that his whole life was about to change. Nor would he necessarily have picked his five fellow heroes of Metru Nui. Vakama was too much of a dreamer, Nokama seemed a little stuck on herself, Matau was simply annoying, and Nuju and Whenua argued constantly.

Still, they must have been chosen for this honor for a reason. Just as a Po-Metru crafter carefully selected the right tools for a job, so the Great Spirit Mata Nui must have had a plan in mind when he chose the six. But what it could be, Onewa had no idea.

Then an awful thought struck him. What if they were not the Matoran meant to become Toa? What if there had been a mistake? An accident? What if one or more of them got Toa stones when they were not meant to do so? What would that mean for Metru Nui?

The idea disturbed him so much that his hand slipped off his proto piton. He caught it, just barely, and decided to stop worrying about what might have been. Things were the way they were. If a crafter got handed a badly made tool to carve, well, he worked with what he was given. Onewa would have to do the same thing.

He was nearing the top now and could see the Great Disk. Getting it out without bringing the slab of protodermis down on top of his head would take skill.

Onewa planted one proto piton, tested to see if it was firm, and then let go of the other. He took hold of the Great Disk and gave a tug, but it wouldn't budge. Another, and another, and still it wasn't going to move.

The Toa of Stone saw only one chance. He was going to have to use both hands. He crawled as far up to the top of the sculpture as he could and let go of the piton. He grabbed the Great Disk with both hands and pulled with all his strength. It gave just a little. Then a little more. One more tug would do it —

It was free!

Onewa felt a split second of triumph. Then he realized the slab was teetering in his direction. That was the good news. He was also falling to the ground, far, far below.

Desperately, he reached out and grabbed one of his pitons. The force of his fall tore it loose from the sculpture, but at least now he had a tool. Now if only he could think of something to do with it.

Down below, Vakama watched Onewa's fall with horror. None of his disks would help in this situation, and melting the slab wouldn't save the Toa of Stone. But there had to be some way his elemental power could help.

Then he remembered something from his lifetime spent around heat and flame. He reached out with his Toa energy and began to heat the air beneath Onewa. Hot air would create an updraft that would slow the Toa's fall, Vakama was almost certain. It wouldn't save him, but it might buy him time to save himself.

Onewa felt his fall slowing slightly as a blanket of warm air surrounded him. He didn't know if it was Vakama giving him this chance or something else, but he was determined not to waste it. He slung his proto piton and caught it on part of the sculpture, twisting his body so he would swing rather than just stop abruptly. The sudden deceleration still felt like it would tear his arm off, but his new Toa strength won out.

He paused to catch his breath and make sure the Great Disk was safe. That's when the shadow fell on him. Onewa looked up to see the massive slab falling right toward him.

He dove headfirst off the sculpture. He tossed his piton ahead of him, felt it catch on the sculpture, and swung around and down. It was now only a short drop to the ground. Onewa hit the sand and rolled, grateful to be back on solid ground.

Then the shadow came again, and he heard Vakama shouting, "Watch out!"

The huge slab of protodermis crashed to the round with a force that sent tremors throughout Po-Metru. When the cloud of sand finally cleared, there stood Onewa, unharmed. Miraculously, the portion of the "mountain" that had come down on him contained the hole that had housed the Great Disk.

From his vantage point, Vakama smiled. Someday, if Onewa allowed it, this would be a wonderful tale to tell.

Vakama, Onewa, Nuhrii and Ahkmou were the first to make it back to the Great Temple. It was Onewa who spotted the squad of Ga-Metru Vahki circling the place.

"What do you think? Could Nokama and Matau be in trouble?" asked Vakama.

Onewa shook his head. "If they had taken two Toa Metru in, the Vahki wouldn't still be here. I'm guessing our friends slipped away and the Vahki are searching the area for them."

"And the other Toa Metru could walk right into their claws. We have to lure them away from here. But what would make Vahki pass up the chance to capture two powerful strangers who appeared in their metru?"

"How about six?" said Onewa, smiling.

"Did I mention this was a bad idea?" asked Nuhrii, trying not to tremble.

"At least eight times," answered Onewa. "It's simple. Just run up to the Vahki and say what we told you."

"Why would they listen to a Ta-Matoran? This is Ga-Metru!"

"Nuhrii, if a Rahi with a slime trail came up to them and told them where to find us, they would listen," said Onewa. "Don't worry. We'd send Ahkmou, but bad things tend to happen whenever he's out my sight."

"Remember, this isn't just about us," said Vakama. "It's for the sake of the whole city."

The Ta-Matoran shrugged. "Yeah. So you keep saying."

Nuhrii dashed out into the avenue and ran straight for the Great Temple. The Vahki immediately flew down and surrounded him. The Toa could not hear what the Matoran was saying, but if he stuck to the script, he was claiming to have seen six strangers on the other end of the metru. They were keeping Matoran from doing their work and generally causing trouble.

As Onewa had expected, that was all the Vahki needed to hear. The Bordakh transformed from bipeds to four-legged creatures, their tools now serving as their front legs. Then they flew off in the direction Nuhrii had pointed. As soon as they were gone, the Ta-Matoran sank to his knees.

Vakama ran over to him. "Good job, Nuhrii."

"You owe me one," said Nuhrii. "You all owe me one."

"Let's hope the city survives long enough for you to collect." Vakama turned at the familiar voice. Nokama was standing behind him with Whenua, Matau, and Nuju, and all were carrying Great Disks. A feeling of relief washed over him — in their first great test, the Toa Metru had succeeded.

"We did as you asked," said Nuju.

"We sought-found the Great Disks," added Matau. "Now what?"

"Tell us how to save the city," said Whenua.

"Ummmm . . . well . . ." Vakama began. His

visions had only shown that the Great Disks were needed to stop the destruction of Metru Nui. The "how" of it had never been revealed.

"Come on, fire-spitter, this was all your idea," snapped Onewa. "We chased all over the city for these things. What are we supposed to do with them?"

"We are supposed to act like Toa," said Nokama. "Vakama put us on the right path. Now we must all decide on the next step. Let us share what we know. Vhisola's researches confirmed what Vakama said — the six Great Disks, used together, can defeat the Morbuzakh. More, it seems there is a single root that is the center of this menace."

"Ehrye showed me records in the Knowledge Tower that refer to a 'king root,'" said Nuju. "It can be recognized by the brown stripe that runs up and down its length."

"But where can it be?" asked Whenua. "It must be huge, to support so many vines over so much distance. Where could such a thing conceal itself?"

"The Archives?" suggested Onewa. "You could hide a Bohrok swarm or three in that place, and still have room for a kolhii disk tournament."

Whenua shook his head. "I'll admit there are a lot of unexplored places down there, but I think we would have noticed evil greenery. What do we know about this thing that might suggest a hiding place?"

"It's strong. It's persistent," Vakama began. "It doesn't seem to like the cold, but thrives in heat. I've never seen anything else survive in a fire pit."

"The Great Furnace," muttered Nuhrii. When the Toa all turned to look at him, he said, "Don't you see? If it loves the heat, what better place to hide?"

"He's right," said the Toa of Fire. "Outside of the fire pits, which are too heavily guarded to provide sanctuary, the Great Furnace is the most significant source of heat in Ta-Metru. If it's driven Matoran away from the area, the Morbuzakh king root could easily conceal itself there."

"Then our course of action is clear," said Nokama. "If there's a chance the root of this menace is in the Great Furnace, then it is to the Great Furnace we shall go. And Vakama will lead us."

"Is that so knowing-wise?" asked Matau. "What makes him any better than the rest?"

Nokama started to answer, but Vakama cut her off. "I'm not interested in being a leader. All I care about is saving the city. Ta-Metru is my home, and I know it better than any of you, so maybe Nokama's right in saying I should be in charge. After we defeat the Morbuzakh, you can all do as you like."

"Too much talking," said Nuju. "Not enough doing. Let's get this over with."

"Any special reason for your hurry?" asked Onewa.

"I hate plants," answered Nuju, as he walked away.

Over their strong objections, the Matoran were going along on the journey to Ta-Metru. Matau had joked that their job would be to keep the king root busy while the Toa waited for the right moment. He assured them that the moment would surely come while at least a few of them were still on their feet. It took Nokama some time to calm them down after that, and she firmly asked Matau to please keep his jokes to himself.

They were traveling along back paths through the city. By now, the Vahki in all six metru had been stirred up and would be watching the chutes. Whenua commented that it was too bad they couldn't change back to Matoran at will, if only to be able to sneak around more effectively.

"You can go back to being a Matoran if you want," Matau had replied. "I like being a Toa-hero!"

By the time they reached the borders of Ga-Metru, Vhisola was looking over her shoulder every few seconds. While the Toa were scanning the air for signs of Vahki, her eyes were fixed on the ground, the shadowy alleys, and anywhere else from which danger might spring.

"What's the matter, Vhisola?" asked Nokama. "You are with six Toa. You will be safe."

"No, I won't," she whispered. "Neither will you, any of you. Don't you know what they say about Morbuzakh vines?"

"Tell me."

"When the Morbuzakh knows you are looking for it —" Vhisola paused and looked around again. Then, in a whisper so soft Nokama could barely hear, she said:

"It comes looking for you."

Just across the northern border of Ta-Metru lay a nearly deserted neighborhood. It had been the site of the first appearances by the Morbuzakh vines. Countless Matoran had disappeared from there, many more had fled for their lives deeper into the metru. Since they entered the area, Vakama had not spoken a word.

"I do not like this place," said Matau, looking around. "It feels cold-dead."

"Where are all the Matoran?" asked Nokama.

"If Ta-Metru is anything like Po-Metru, they are living now with friends or co-workers," answered Onewa. "Some insist on staying near the Vahki hives, believing it to be safer there. If they work near the outskirts, they're careful not to travel alone. Every few moments, they stop working to listen for the approach of a vine."

Whenua frowned. "There was nothing in the past history of Metru Nui to hint such a crisis might occur."

"But something like it was bound to happen," said Nuju. "We relied too much on others to protect us — Toa, Vahki, even Turaga Dume. When something happened they could not handle, all the Matoran could do was run. I could have predicted this."

"Then why didn't you?" asked Vakama, gesturing at the abandoned buildings all around. "Why didn't anyone?"

"I predict we better find a place to hide," broke in Onewa. "There's a Vahki squad up ahead."

"This way." Vakama led his fellow Toa Metru and the six Matoran into a narrow alleyway. Using his flame power, he melted the lock on an old door and shepherded them inside the building.

The heat struck the Toa like a fist. Although no Matoran seemed to be present in the forge, fires still leaped high and smoke made it hard to breathe. Tools were scattered about at the work stations and some items had even been left to melt in the flames.

"They left in a hurry," said Whenua. "Maybe we should do the same."

The Toa of Ice felt something strike his armor and bounce off. It made a sharp sound when it hit, as if it were a pebble. When it happened a second time, Nuju said, "What is that?"

Nokama's keen eyes had spotted where the second object landed. She bent down and scooped it up. It was a round object, roughly a quarter of the diameter of a Kanoka disk. Its outer shell was pitted, extremely hard, and the colors of fire. "It looks like some kind of . . . seed."

Another fell, and then another. That's when the full impact of what she had just said became clear to her. She looked up at the ceiling. It was covered in seeds, which were beginning to fall at a rapid pace. "Oh, Mata Nui protect us," she whispered. "Morbuzakh seeds! It must be!"

Now the Toa Metru were caught in a

downpour. When the seeds struck, tiny vines sprang forth from the shell and wrapped around whatever was closest, hanging on with an unnatural strength.

"We have to get out of here!" Vakama shouted. He took two steps before black-brown tendrils wrapped around his legs, bringing him down hard. More seeds struck him, their vines binding him as effectively as chains. He could see the other Toa struggling, their arms pinned to their sides, their tools out of reach, as more seeds rained down.

The clatter of the shells striking the ground was deafening. Already, the stone floor was covered with a layer of rapidly germinating seeds. The little vines writhed like a nest of baby serpents, striking out to entangle the Toa. Nokama was in the worst shape, with vines covering her from neck to toe and reaching for her Mask of Power.

None of the six Matoran had made it back out the door. They were pinned to the walls by tendrils, like insects caught in a blackened web.

Vakama rolled across the floor, trying to find a sharp-edged fragment of protodermis he could use to saw through the vines. Whenua was on his feet, slamming his body against the wall, evidently trying to stun the plants into letting go.

But it was Nuju who first managed to escape. Nokama's eyes widened as she saw him slice through the vines binding him with an icicle. In mere moments he was free and rushing over to help her. "We have to get the others out of here. Help me!"

While Nuju hurried to untie the other Toa, Nokama used her hydro blades to free the Matoran. Then they all rushed out the door before the vines could grab hold again. Vakama slammed the door shut behind them, stamping on the vines as they tried to slip underneath. "Nuju! Onewa! Bring the building down!"

Onewa called on his elemental energies as Nuju did the same. From one side of the building, a pillar of stone rose into the air. From the other, a pillar of ice took shape. Nodding to each other, both Toa released their control and sent the twin pillars crashing into the roof. Under the weight of rock and ice, the forge collapsed in on itself, burying the plants.

Nokama felt a shudder run through her form. "Do you think that will stop them?"

Vakama shook his head. "Maybe for a little while. You know what this means, don't you?"

"It's reproducing," said Whenua, "and we have no idea how many other seeds might be waiting to sprout. Their roots will link up with the king root and the Morbuzakh will be everywhere."

"It could overrun our city-home," Matau said quietly. "Too many vines to stop, too little time."

Vakama checked to make sure his disk launcher was loaded. Then he turned to the group and said, "Let's go. We have a weed to pull."

As they walked, Nokama turned to Nuju. "I appreciate your rescue. But how did you get free?"

"I saw what the seeds were doing to the

others," he said, his eyes looking straight ahead. "So when they began to strike me, I took a deep breath and expanded my chest. Then when I let the breath out, I had just enough slack to move a little. I didn't need my spikes to make something as simple as an icicle."

"That's amazing!"

Nuju shrugged. "I'm from Ko-Metru. We think ahead."

The Great Furnace was not as big or imposing as the Coliseum in the center of Metru Nui. It did not have the feeling of power and mystery that Ga-Metru's Great Temple possessed. But every Ta-Matoran looked at it with awe and wonder. It was a symbol of what made the metru great — the power that turned solid protodermis to molten liquid, and the skill to shape that raw material into the tools Matoran used every day.

Now Vakama stood outside the entrance, staring up at the reddish-black exterior, wondering just what was lurking in the heart of the flame.

"So this is the plan?" asked Onewa in disbelief. "We knock on the front door and ask if the Morbuzakh can come out to play?"

"I am not saying we should listen to all of Vhisola's fears," replied Nokama, making an effort to remain calm. "But if she is right —"

"If she is right, then we are facing more than just a plant," said Matau. "It can think-plan. And it probably already knows we're here."

"Then we won't keep it waiting," said Vakama. "Nuhrii, you and the other Matoran will accompany us inside, but stay back. There is no telling what we will encounter in there."

"One of us should stay out here to run for help, if need be," offered Ahkmou. "I volunteer."

"If we fail," said Onewa, "Metru Nui will be beyond help. Besides, you were so anxious to get the six Great Disks, Ahkmou, I think you should see them in action."

The six Toa Metru looked at each other. The time for talking had passed. Each knew that the challenges they had faced so far could not compare with what they were about to attempt.

No one needed to say that this might be the last adventure for one or more of them. Their good-byes to each other were exchanged in silence.

Vakama melted the lock on the massive door. With a final look at his friends, he opened the gateway to the Great Furnace.

Toa and Matoran entered the structure. Just inside the door was a small, bare chamber. Its purpose was to give Matoran a chance to prepare before they proceeded to the inferno inside, or give them a chance to rest after they had spent some time laboring in the furnace. Beyond this chamber was the outer ring, a buffer to keep the intense heat from reaching the outer walls of the building.

Surprisingly, there was no sign of the Morbuzakh here. A moment of panic swept through Vakama. What if they had been wrong? What if the king root was not here?

Then we find it, wherever it hides, he said to himself. *There's no other choice.*

He grasped the handle of the door to the outer ring. Vakama could feel the heat through it. In his mind, he was prepared for almost anything on the other side of that door. But in his heart, he wondered if six new, still untried Toa Metru would have the power to prevail.

Disk launcher ready, Vakama threw open the door and rushed inside. Dim lightstones cast an unsettling glow on the long, narrow chamber. The air was filled with a strange, soft sound that seemed to come from everywhere at once.

"What is that?" asked Vakama. "It sounds like hissing."

"No, not hissing," replied Nokama. "It's . . . whispering."

The Toa Metru stopped dead and looked around. The stone floor of the chamber was broken in numerous places. Growing from the cracks were small, twisted plants, with buds that stank of rot. Close inspection showed the buds were pulsating.

"It's them. The sounds are coming from them," Whenua said. "Are they —"

Onewa stepped carefully, trying to avoid touching any of the plants. "Yes. They're young

Morbuzakh. New vines growing to strangle the city."

The whispering grew louder. The children of the Morbuzakh sensed that they were not alone. A few of the plants began to stir, as if in a breeze. Then more started moving as agitation spread throughout the outer ring.

"We cannot allow these things to grow-thrive," said Matau.

"Let's see how they like a touch of frost." Nuju lowered his crystal spikes and sprayed a fine mist of ice over the plants. As the Toa watched, the ice spread across the entire crop. The plants began to sag beneath the weight, their whispering growing louder, then fainter. Finally, all was silent.

Nokama took a step forward and water splashed around her feet. "Nuju! The heat in here is melting your ice."

"Then I'll make more," said the Toa of Ice. He poured more and more of his energy through his tools, creating layer after layer of frost on top of the plants. Each time the heat of the Great Furnace would melt the ice and the plants would begin to struggle again. Then Nuju would call on more of his power.

The seesaw battle between Toa Metru and the flames of Ta-Metru went on for several long minutes. The other Toa could see that Nuju was weakening. He staggered and would have fallen if Matau had not caught him.

"My power . . . almost gone . . ." gasped Nuju.

This was a mistake, thought Vakama. *Our true struggle is waiting beyond this chamber. We should have saved our power for that. But why would the Morbuzakh leave these young vines undefended?*

The Toa of Fire got his answer in the next moment. Wave after wave of thorns flew from the walls, knifing through the air at the Toa Metru. "Toa! Defend yourselves!" Vakama shouted, hurling firebursts to incinerate the projectiles.

Whenua yelled as one of the thorns grazed his armor. He activated his earthshock drills and began shredding the thorns as they came close.

Across the chamber, Matau was conjuring a wind funnel to blow the thorns away, while Nokama used her hydro blades to parry them. Onewa was having the most trouble, but he stood and let the thorns strike him to buy the Matoran time to seek shelter.

The six Matoran had hit the ground and were scrambling through the melted ice toward the door. Nuhrii glanced up and saw that the hail of thorns was heaviest near the exit. "We'll never make it!"

"We have to," said Ahkmou. "I'm not staying here!"

"Be quiet, Ahkmou!" snapped Tehutti. "We might not be here if it weren't for you. I saw something in the Archives once that might help us. Everyone join hands!"

The other five Matoran did as Tehutti asked. "Now concentrate," the Onu-Matoran said. "We have to focus on our unity. That means you too, Ahkmou!"

At first, their efforts seemed to be have no effect. Then a glow surrounded the six Matoran and their bodies grew hazy and indistinct. There was a sudden, bright burst of light, and when it faded, one Matoran stood where six had been before.

"We are one," the being said in a voice that sounded like a combination of the six Matoran. "We are the Matoran Nui."

The eyes of the merged being scanned the chamber. The Toa Metru were fighting for their lives against the thorn barrage, but making no progress. "We understand now," said the Matoran Nui. "No one Matoran's ambitions are more important than Metru Nui as a whole. We must aid the Toa."

The Matoran Nui darted forward, moving so quickly it dodged the thorns. Then with one blow it demolished the door to the inner chamber. The Toa Metru turned at the noise to stare in amazement at the new being in their midst.

"Go!" said the Matoran Nui. "Defeat the Morbuzakh and save the city! It is what you were meant to do!"

Vakama had a million questions, but no

time to ask any of them. He turned to the other Toa and shouted, "Follow me!"

The six heroes of Metru Nui charged into the heart of the Great Furnace toward what might be their final conflict. The Matoran Nui watched them go, whispering, "Mata Nui protect you all."

Outside of the Great Furnace, the Matoran Nui split apart to become six Matoran again. They blinked and stumbled, drained from their experience. "That was incredible. The power!" said Ehrye.

"Let's do it again," said Vhisola. "Think of all we could do for our city."

Ahkmou shook his head and backed away. "No. No. No way. If you five want to risk your lives, go ahead, but count me out. I'm looking out for what's most important: me."

"Then go," said Tehutti. "If unity, duty, and destiny mean nothing to you, run back to Po-Metru, Ahkmou."

The Po-Matoran laughed. "We'll see each other again. Don't worry. And then we will see just whose destiny will win out."

With that, Ahkmou turned and fled into the shadows.

The Toa Metru stood in the midst of a nightmare.

The massive inner chamber of the Great Furnace had been transformed into a sanctuary for the king root of the Morbuzakh. Dominating the room was a huge, thick, winding stalk that extended from the ground all the way to the rooftop. The winding stripe that ran down its length marked it as the source of the Morbuzakh plague.

Branches extended all along the root, entwining themselves with the masonry of the walls and floors. The king root had truly become a part of the Great Furnace. The Toa Metru could imagine each of those branches extending beyond the furnace, with multiple vines sprouting from them to threaten Metru Nui.

Waves and waves of intense heat washed over the Toa. Already Nuju and Whenua were beginning to weaken. Vakama turned to the Toa of Water, saying, "Nokama, you must use your power to try to keep us cool. Can you do it?"

"I don't know," replied Nokama. "I will do my best."

The Toa of Water concentrated, calling on her energies to condense the moisture in the air into a cooling mist. It was an enormous drain, with the heat taking its toll on her as well. She could not help but wonder how long her strength would hold out, and what would happen if she fell.

Vakama felt overwhelmed. The king root was far bigger and more frightening than he had ever dreamed. How could six disks, even Great Disks, bring such a monstrosity down? But what choice did they have?

"Ready the disks," he said. "We will strike together and —"

"Noooo!" The voice cracked like lightning in the minds of the Toa. "You will not desssstroy the Morbuzakh!"

"What? Who was that?" said Onewa, looking around.

"It wasssss I!" the voice boomed again.

"Mata Nui," whispered Nokama. "It's the Morbuzakh — it speaks!"

"Yessss, I sssspeak. I ssspeak. I think. I feel. And Metru Nui sssshall be mine!"

Vakama could see no eyes or mouth anywhere on the root. It was not truly speaking, the Toa were simply hearing its thoughts. Worse, they could sense its feelings — an overwhelming hunger to possess the city and drive away anything that was not Morbuzakh. There was more there as well, traces of another intelligence, but they were too vague for the Toa to comprehend.

"My armssss extend to every part of thissss city," the Morbuzakh continued. "I am in the furnacesss, the canalsss, the chutesss. The Matoran live and work only because I choossse to let them. But if they anger me —"

A vine suddenly shot out of the wall, wrapped around a pipe, and crushed it to dust. "Firsst, I will drive the Matoran away from the outskirtsss of the city, so they cannot essscape. Then I will claim this place as my own. Those who ssssurvive can ssserve the Morbuzakh, or perisssh."

The full horror of what they were hearing struck the Toa then. This was no mere overgrown menace, like the wild Rahi beasts that sometimes appeared in the city. The Morbuzakh was intelligent, cunning, and evil beyond anything they had ever imagined. None of them doubted that, if allowed to spread unchecked, this thing would do what it promised. Metru Nui would fall and the Matoran would become slaves of the Morbuzakh, or worse.

So shocked were the Toa Metru that none of them noticed a vine creeping up behind Whenua. It struck amazingly fast, ripping the Great Disk from the Toa's grasp and snaking up toward the ceiling. Whenua shouted and grabbed the vine, which lifted him high into the air.

Nuju ran, leaped, and caught Whenua's legs. He, too, was yanked off his feet and up toward the ceiling. The Morbuzakh vine whipped around violently in an effort to shake the Toa off. "Hang on!" shouted Nuju.

"Thanks! That was my plan!" said Whenua. "Did you come up here just to tell me that?"

Down below, vines had wrapped themselves around Vakama and Onewa, but Matau had proven too fast for them. The Toa of Air darted across the floor, heading straight for the king root. "Morbuzakh, meet a Toa-hero!"

Before Matau's startled eyes, a new vine grew out of the root. Before he could change direction, the vine swatted him out of the air and sent him crashing into the wall.

Nokama, still straining to maintain her power, watched as Vakama's fire and Onewa's stone failed to make the vines break their grip. Above, Nuju had called upon his ice power but it was too weak to free him and Whenua.

This is all wrong, she thought. *We are all fighting individual battles, instead of working as a team. There has to be a way to stop this thing!*

Ignoring the possible consequences, Nokama suddenly dropped her efforts to keep the Toa cool amid the awful heat. She fired a stream of water up toward the vine that held Whenua's Great Disk, shouting, "Nuju! Freeze this!"

The Toa of Ice did as she asked, forming the curving stream of water into an ice hook. Reaching out and grabbing it, he used the ice to pull the end of the vine close. "Whenua! Now!"

Whenua thrust his earthshock drill forward and sliced through the vine. The portion holding the Great Disk fell away and plunged toward the ground as the vine writhed.

Nokama glanced at Matau, who had finally regained his feet. Her eyes met his and she knew he was ready. He raised his aero slicers and hurled a blast of air at the falling vine, blowing it toward Nokama. The Toa of Water caught it on the fly, tore the vine loose, and held the Great Disk up proudly.

"Your first defeat, monster!" she shouted at the king root. "But hardly your last!"

"You can delay me, but not defeat me!" The Morbuzakh's voice sounded like a swarm of metallic hornets. "I am a part of Metru Nui now. I am thisss city, and it isss me!"

"Then we will tear you out by the roots, Morbuzakh!" Vakama shouted. "One way or another, your reign ends today!"

The vine holding Vakama swung him close to the body of the king root. Vakama took the opportunity to toss fireballs at the Morbuzakh, but the plant simply absorbed them. "Yesssss," said the Morbuzakh. "More! Fire feedssss me!"

Whenua looked down at Matau, who nodded. Then the Toa of Earth let go of the vine, sending Nuju and himself plummeting toward the ground. When they were midway through their fall, Matau sent two mighty gusts of wind toward them. The wind caught the two Toa and flung them across the chamber right at the vines holding Vakama and Onewa.

Toa of Ice and Toa of Earth slammed into the vines. The impact freed the two trapped Toa, who dropped to the ground. They had no chance to rest, however — Morbuzakh vines were now coming from every side, trying to grab the Toa or their Great Disks.

Now began a desperate struggle, for the Toa Metru were not facing just one powerful, if immobile, enemy. They were fighting the thousand "arms" of the Morbuzakh, each as strong as the last, which struck and then slithered away. Toa tools flashed. Fire, ice, water, stone, earth, and cyclones filled the air. But for every vine the Toa struck down, three more rose to take its place.

Eventually, the Toa began to tire. Without extensive practice in controlling and rationing their elemental energies, their powers began to run low. Little by little, the vines drove them away from the king root, growing bolder as they sensed the Toa slowing down.

"You cannot sssstop me," hissed the Morbuzakh. "You have not the ssstrength. That isss all right. Too weak to be heroesss, perhapsss, but you will ssstill make excellent ssslavesss."

"He's right," said Vakama. "We can't win this way."

Onewa drove off another vine and looked at the Toa of Fire in disbelief. "This was your idea, and now you're quitting? What kind of a Toa are you?"

"Stop fighting," Vakama said flatly. "It's our only chance."

"You have gone around the chute," said Matau. "We stop hard-fighting and the vines will overwhelm us and drag us to the —" The Toa of Air suddenly stopped and a broad smile appeared on his face. "For a fire-spitter, Vakama, sometimes you can be almost as quick-smart as a Le-Matoran."

Vakama checked to make sure that all the Toa had their Great Disks in their hands. Then he shouted, "Now!" As one, they dropped their Toa tools and stopped struggling against the vines.

At first, the Morbuzakh did not seem to know how to react. When the king root spoke in their minds, there was confusion in its tone. "You would not sssurrender. Thisss is sssome trick. My vinesss could crusssh you where you ssstand!"

"Then do it," said Nokama. "Don't just talk about it."

"Maybe when we are done here, we could transplant this thing to Ga-Metru," Whenua suggested. "You know, add it to the garden near the canals. Ga-Matoran could climb it and build root-houses."

"As long as it stops speaking," said Nuju. "There is nothing I dislike more than a talkative shrub."

"Do what you like, Morbuzakh," snapped Onewa. "I would rather be fed to the Great Furnace than live in a city run by an obnoxious, foul-smelling, overgrown pile of vegetable matter good for nothing but clogging canals."

The Morbuzakh's bellow was so loud the Toa thought sure their heads would split open. Six vines shot around and wrapped around the heroes' waists, hauling them through the air toward the king root. The pressure of the vines was tremendous, threatening to squeeze the air out of the Toa's lungs.

"Before you ssserve, you will sssuffer!"

Vakama held up his Great Disk as the other Toa did the same. "No, Morbuzakh. You have had your season. The time for the harvest has come!"

Pure power flashed from the six Great Disks, blindingly bright bands of energy that twisted around each other. Lightning flashed wherever two bands touched, striking at the vines that reached for the Toa. Then the energies blended together, forming a sphere in mid-air that moved slowly and inexorably toward the Morbuzakh.

Desperately, the Morbuzakh tried to escape its own end. It writhed, the sheer power of its vines pulling down the walls of the Great Furnace. Masonry rained down from the ceiling as the plant's upper branches tried to batter their way to freedom. Great blocks of protodermis crumbled and fell into the flames, consumed in an instant, and still the Morbuzakh struggled. It had truly become one with this fortress of fire, and now both were about to fall.

Taking advantage of the distraction, the Toa fought their way free of the vines that imprisoned them. Vakama looked up and saw that power no longer flowed from his Great Disk, nor from any of the others. But the sphere still existed, growing larger and larger every moment.

"Toa, we have to go! Now!" he shouted. "The Morbuzakh will bring the Great Furnace down upon us!"

Then came a sound the Toa Metru would remember for the rest of their lives: the sound of the king root screaming.

That put an end to any arguments there might have been. Instead, the Toa raced for the exit to the outer chamber, pausing only to pick up their tools. They did not stop running until they were far from the Great Furnace and the thing that had dwelled inside.

Only Vakama dared to look back. Through the crumbling walls, he could see that the energy sphere now encompassed the king root. Its walls had sliced through the multitude of vines, the high branches, and the deep roots that anchored the Morbuzakh in the ground. All around, the plant growth that had menaced Metru Nui was writhing and crumbling to dust.

The king root hung suspended in the air now, trapped within the energy sphere. Cut off from the ground below and from its branches and vines, the root could no longer draw energy from the fires of Ta-Metru or feed it to the rest of the plant. It was alive, but isolated, a creature once connected with all of Metru Nui and now utterly alone. Eventually, its howls of rage began to fade away in the minds of the Toa, replaced by the sound of their own thoughts.

The Great Furnace was now nothing but rubble and flames. The sphere glowed amid the wreckage as the struggles of the king root ceased. Then, as suddenly as it had appeared, the energy was gone. The king root struck the ground with a resounding crash and then crumbled to nothing before the Toa of Fire's astounded eyes.

* * *

All around the city, Matoran looked on in wonder as the Morbuzakh vines turned to dust. Soon, there would be no sign of the plant left, except for the damage it had done. But the defeat of the Morbuzakh would not bring back all the Matoran who had vanished since the vines had first appeared in Metru Nui.

Back at the ruins of the Great Furnace, Nokama looked at Vakama. "Is it really over?"

"Yes," said the Toa of Fire. "With the king root gone, the rest of the Morbuzakh should soon follow. We have passed our first test as Toa Metru."

"Then why are we standing here?" asked Matau. "Let's bring these ever-powerful disks to the Coliseum and tell the world we are Toa-heroes!"

The six Toa Metru looked at each other and smiled. Matau's idea sounded like a good one. After all, despite their differences, they had found the Great Disks, defeated the Morbuzakh, and saved their city. As they walked away from the site of their first great victory, they knew they were no longer the Matoran they had been . . . or even the new Toa they had become . . .

They were heroes of Metru Nui.

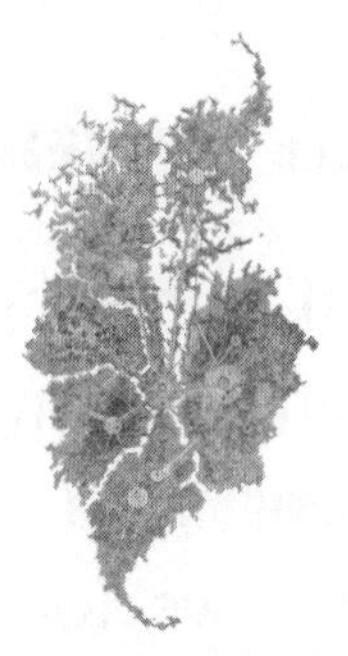

EPILOGUE

Turaga Vakama rose, signaling that his tale had come to an end. Takanuva, the Toa of Light, stood as well, smiling. "What a wonderful story!" he said. "The six of you started out as Matoran, just like I did, and became heroes. I bet the whole city turned out to cheer for you!"

Vakama chuckled. "You are attaching a happy ending to my tale, Takanuva, because you wish there to be one. But there is much more to tell."

"You had a vision when you first became a Toa," said Tahu, Toa of Fire. "A vision of disaster. Did defeating the Morbuzakh spare the city from that terrible event?"

"It spared the city from the Morbuzakh," said Turaga Vakama. "We believed that was enough. Our world was very simple, Tahu, with good on one side and evil on the other."

"What's wrong with that?" asked Onua, Toa of Earth. "I mean, we Toa challenged the Rahi and many other threats to this island. We fought for justice and to defend the Matoran and their villages. We stood up for the light and defeated the darkness that rose against us."

"You are very wise, Onua," said Vakama. "But you have only the wisdom of your experience. That is why you are here now — to gain the wisdom of mine."

There was an uncomfortable silence, broken finally by Takanuva. "It's late. I suppose we should leave Turaga Vakama to his rest. There will be time tomorrow for another tale. There is another tale to tell, isn't there, Turaga?"

"Oh, yes, Takanuva," said Vakama. *A dark one indeed,* he added to himself.

The Toa departed, all but Gali, Toa of Water. She had always been sensitive to others' moods, and she could tell that Vakama was troubled. It was more than just confronting the memories of his past. It seemed as if there were some terrible secret he knew he must share, but dreaded doing so.

"Why do you tell these tales, Turaga?" she asked softly. "Is it only to prepare us for the journey to Metru Nui, and what we may encounter there?"

"You already know the answer," he said, "or you would not ask the question. No, there is a great difference between the Toa Nuva that you are, and the Toa Metru that we Turaga were long ago. Your enemies hide in the shadows, but you know they are there. They make no effort to hide the darkness in their hearts. For us, it was . . . different."

"But you were strong," she said. "You triumphed. You had the three virtues to guide you — Unity, Duty, Destiny."

"Yes, we six had done our duty, we believed," Vakama said, with a trace of sadness in his voice. "And we felt certain we had achieved our destiny. But our unity? That still remained to be forged in the fires of danger, far greater danger than we had known before."

Vakama leaned on his firestaff. Not for the first time, Gali found it hard to believe that the Turaga had once been a mighty Toa Metru. "You see, Toa of Water, we believed that we knew all we needed to know to be heroes. We could challenge an enemy, outwit it, defeat it, save Matoran, even save a city. Oh, we still needed training in our powers and we still had to master our masks. But being a hero? There was nothing left for us to learn there, we felt sure."

Vakama looked at Gali. She understood now that his eyes had seen a greater darkness than any Toa Nuva could comprehend. *What happened on Metru Nui?* she wondered.

"We thought we knew it all. But we were wrong, Gali, so very wrong. Our true lessons were about to begin."

BIONICLE®

The Darkness Below

For Leah, who brings style, class,
and grace to everything she does

INTRODUCTION

Jaller paused from his labors for a moment and took a deep breath. He could not remember ever working harder than he had in the past few days. Ever since it had been announced that the Matoran were going to move from the island of Mata Nui to the island city of Metru Nui, villagers had been toiling day and night to build enough boats for the great journey.

For Jaller and his friends, the nonstop work was welcome. Their home, Ta-Koro, had been destroyed in the battle to save the island from darkness, and they were living in other villages until the time came to leave Mata Nui forever. Talk around the fires at night was about Metru Nui, what wonders they might find there, and how soon they would be able to leave for this new and mysterious place.

"We'll never get to Metru Nui if the great Jaller keeps taking rest breaks."

Jaller turned to see his friend Hahli smiling at him. The Ga-Matoran had recently been named the new Chronicler, and ever since she had been traveling from place to place gathering tales about Metru Nui. She hoped to be able to share the stories with the other Matoran during the long journey to come.

"At least when I'm working, I'm *working,*" replied Jaller good-naturedly. "You can't build a boat with a story, you know."

"Maybe not, but it sure makes the sailing go faster. I'm heading to see Turaga Vakama. He's about to continue his tale of Metru Nui to the Toa. I am supposed to record it for the Wall of History we will build on the new island. Come with me?"

Jaller thought about it. He probably should keep working, but he was already far ahead of all the others. It wouldn't do any harm to take a little time off.

"Okay. Let's go," he said.

The two of them set out for the Amaja Circle sandpit, the place where Turaga Vakama traditionally told his tales. After a short while, Jaller asked, "So is it true?"

"Is what true?"

"All the stories I have been hearing. How the Turaga were once Toa on Metru Nui; how they searched for six missing Matoran, but learned that one of the Matoran planned to betray the city; and how they gathered six Great Disks and used them to defeat a menace called the Morbuzakh."

Hahli nodded. "Yes, it's all true. Amazing, isn't it? One moment, they were Matoran just like us, living and working in a great city. The next moment, they were Toa Metru with powers and Toa tools and everything!"

Up ahead, they could see the seven Toa gathered around Turaga Vakama. The Turaga had already begun to speak. "It had been a difficult and dangerous mission, but we six Toa Metru had triumphed. Metru Nui had been saved from the Morbuzakh, and we were certain that we would be hailed as heroes. But we were about to face another test, one that would threaten to shatter our newfound unity."

The Turaga of Fire turned his gaze to the night sky, but all present knew that his eyes were truly viewing images from the past. "Toa would challenge Toa in the darkness below the city, in a struggle that still lives in my nightmares."

The six Toa Metru walked through the streets of Ta-Metru, on their way to the Coliseum. For the first time since they had transformed from Matoran, they felt no need to travel by way of back alleys or to stay in the shadows. Even the presence of Vahki, Metru Nui's order enforcement squads, did not worry them. After all, they had just defeated the Morbuzakh plant that menaced the city. They were heroes!

Better still, they had found the legendary Great Disks, which had been hidden in separate parts of the city. They had no doubt that these artifacts would be enough to convince the city's elder, Turaga Dume, and all the Matoran that here were new Toa capable of defeating any threat.

"They will cheer-hail us in the Coliseum," said Matau, Toa of Air, with a grin. "Po-Metru carvers will make statues of us. Perhaps they will even rename the districts for us! 'Ma-Metru' — I like the ring-sound of that!"

The other Toa laughed. Matau was exaggerating, of course, but certainly Turaga Dume would honor them in some way. Matoran all over the city would demand it.

"With the Morbuzakh gone, maybe we won't have any dangers to face," offered Whenua, Toa of Earth. "Except for the occasional Rahi beast on the loose, Metru Nui is usually pretty peaceful."

"Just rest on our reputations, huh, Whenua?" said Onewa, Toa of Stone. "Not me. Now that I'm a Toa Metru, I'm going to take advantage of it. The best tools, the best materials, mine for the asking — I'll build statues like you have never seen before!"

"I will do many Toa-hero deeds," said Matau. "That way there will always be tales to tell about me. What about you, Nokama?"

"Well, I'm not sure," replied the Toa of Water. "There are so many places to see and explore. What is it like under the sea? What lies beyond the sky? Where do all those strange creatures you see in the Onu-Metru Archives come from? Now I have the power to go wherever I please and learn those answers."

Nuju, Toa of Ice, shrugged. "I don't feel any need to explore. I have more than enough to keep me busy in Ko-Metru. Now that I am a Toa, perhaps others will not be so quick to interrupt me when I am working."

Only Vakama, Toa of Fire, had yet to speak. Of all the Toa Metru, he was the least comfortable with his new powers and the responsibilities that came with them. Still, when duty demanded it, he had risen to the occasion and led the Toa to victory. Nokama noticed his silence and asked, "What about you, Vakama? Surely you have some dream you want to realize now that you are a Toa?"

"Not really," he answered. "I mean, I am glad we became Toa and were able to save the city. But . . . I would be just as happy to still be working at my forge in Ta-Metru. It was much simpler. I guess once a mask-maker, always a mask-maker."

Onewa chuckled. "The fire-spitter wants to go back to being a Matoran. I don't think the transformation works in the opposite direction."

"Yes, we are stuck being Toa-heroes," said Matau. "And so many worry-problems we have — how many bows to take? How many mask-sculptures in each metru? How big of a shelter-house for each of us?"

"If you aren't happy being a Toa, Vakama, maybe we should choose a new leader," said Onewa. "I am sure I could do the job."

"Or I!" said Matau. "Matau of Ma-Metru, leader of the Toa-heroes! Oh, I like that!"

"I never said I didn't want to be a Toa," Vakama said. "And I *never* said I wanted to be the leader. I did the job because I knew Ta-Metru better than any of you. If someone else wants to be leader, go ahead."

Nokama looked at Vakama. She could tell that he was hurt by the things Onewa and Matau were saying, but he wasn't going to admit to it. As they walked, the other Toa Metru debated who was best qualified to lead the team. Onewa said it should be a creative thinker like him. Matau countered that a high-flyer was best qualified to plan strategy. Whenua said he would take the job if asked, then seemed disappointed when no one asked him.

As for Nuju, the Toa of Ice summed up his feelings in a few words. "I don't care who leads us, as long as he doesn't expect me to follow."

Nokama was about to put all four of them in their place when she saw a Matoran approaching at a run. He was from Onu-Metru, and the anxious look on his face said there was serious trouble somewhere.

Whenua stepped forward to greet him. The Matoran's name was Nuparu, and he was not someone Whenua knew well. When other workers in the Archives were busy among the exhibits, Nuparu was off on his own tinkering. He was always trying to figure out how Gukko birds flew, how the great Muaka cat could stretch its neck to lunge at prey, and other questions that might seem trivial to others. Still, Nuparu leaving the Archives and hurrying into Ta-Metru was enough to catch the Toa of Earth's attention.

"Toa! The Archives are in danger!" the Matoran shouted.

"It's all right, Nuparu," said Whenua. "The Morbuzakh has been defeated. Everyone is safe."

The Matoran shook his head frantically. "No, no, it's not the Morbuzakh. It's the sea! It's going to flood the Archives and destroy all of the exhibits!"

Whenua wasn't sure how to react to the Matoran's words. The Onu-Metru digging machines, and the workers who operated them, took special care to make sure the outer walls of the Archives were reinforced. The deeper they dug to create new sublevels, the greater the pressure from the liquid protodermis outside. But the sea had never posed a serious threat to the existence of the exhibits in all of Metru Nui's recorded history.

The Toa of Earth waved the other Toa Metru away. This was an Onu-Metru problem, and would be solved by the guardian of that district, he decided. "Now tell me what you saw," he said to Nuparu.

"I was down . . . um . . . below the sub-levels, and —"

"Wait a moment, what were you doing so far down? You know how risky it is to go there!" As soon as he said it, Whenua regretted the sharpness of his tone. But it had not been so long ago that he had been down in that dark and fearsome section, and he had barely escaped intact. No Onu-Matoran, archivist or not, had any business wandering among "exhibits" deemed too dangerous for display.

"Well, I . . . I . . . I heard there was a Rahkshi down there, a yellow one, and it had been defeated, and I wanted to . . . well . . ."

"You were hoping to scavenge some parts for your latest invention," Whenua finished for him, frowning. "You know what would happen if the other archivists caught you doing that? Or worse, a Vahki?"

"I know," Nuparu said, looking down at his

feet. "But I didn't find anything anyway. Then I saw a hatch in the floor and I went down through it. There was a whole maze of tunnels there I never knew existed! So I used my lightstone to explore. I didn't see very much, no exhibits or anything, but when I rounded a corner, I was suddenly walking in protodermis! The sea was leaking in!"

Nuparu's voice was loud enough that the other Toa Metru could not help but hear. Nokama, in particular, was intrigued by the mention of the sea. She drew closer as the Matoran continued to talk.

"So at first I didn't know what to think. I was going to turn back, but then I figured as long as I was down there, I'd better find out how serious the situation was. I found one whole wall had a huge crack and the sea was pouring right through it!"

"How bad?"

"The crack is spreading. If it's not repaired soon, the whole sea wall will breach," said Nuparu. "The sublevels will flood, then the lower levels, and pretty soon the whole Archives will be washed away."

"But there is a repair crew headed down now, right?"

Nuparu shook his head. "No one wants to go down there. They've all heard too many stories. That's why, when I heard there was a new Toa of Earth, I came looking for you. Someone has to do something!"

"Someone will," replied Whenua. "Now tell me the story again. I want to hear every detail of what you saw, and where you saw it."

Nokama had rejoined the others by the time Whenua was finished talking with the Matoran. The Toa of Earth looked grim as he walked over to the group.

"I have to go," he said. "Someone will have to apologize to Turaga Dume for me, but this is an emergency. I'll meet you all at the Coliseum later on."

"What could be more serious-matter than telling the world what we can do?" asked Matau.

"Actually doing it," Nokama answered. "But you don't have to take on this task alone. I will come with you. The Archives are important to everyone in Metru Nui. I know anyone from Ga-Metru would do the same."

"I'll come too," said Vakama. "My flame power is weak after the struggle with the Morbuzakh, but maybe I can help somehow." He turned to Onewa. "Can you three explain to Turaga Dume why we cannot present ourselves to him just yet?"

"Oh, sure," Onewa snorted. "'The other three of us would be here, Turaga, but they're out being heroes while we stand around.' I say we *all* go, we *all* do the job, and then we *all* head to the Coliseum. What do you think? Matau? Nuju?"

"The sooner we take care of all this, the sooner I can get back to Ko-Metru," said Nuju. "I say we help Whenua."

"Hmmmmmm," Matau said. "I was in a hurry to tell the Matoran we are Toa-heroes now. But I suppose repair-saving the Archives along with the whole city will be good for twice the celebration. On to Onu-Metru!"

Their course of action agreed upon, the six changed direction and began journeying toward the metru of the archivists. Whenua led the way, still talking with Nuparu, while Nokama and Vakama brought up the rear. After a short while, the Toa of Water said, "You know, we cannot take a vote every time we have to decide something."

"What's that?"

"Just now. The protodermis could have risen another level in the time it took for each Toa to decide if he was coming along or not. We don't have the luxury of debating every point. We need a leader."

"I'm sure you'll do a fine job," he said.

"No, that's not what I —" Nokama began, but the Toa of Fire had already walked away.

Whenua led the Toa Metru to a desolate spot just inside the border of Onu-Metru. Most of the chutes and much of the aboveground structure of the Archives had been damaged by Morbuzakh vines, and Onu-Matoran were now hard at work doing repairs. All of them stopped their labors at the sight of the Toa and crowded around.

Matau greeted them warmly and immediately launched into a tale of the Toa's heroic deeds. The other Toa watched, amused, as he turned their clash with the Morbuzakh into an even greater adventure than it had been.

"If he wasn't a Toa, he could apply to be Chronicler," Onewa said. "Is he ever quiet?"

"Not that you would notice," said Nokama. "Whenua, I don't see an entrance to the Archives here. How will we get where we have to go?"

"There's no entrance you can see," Whenua said. He walked down an alleyway and knelt beside an iron ring in the pavement. He grabbed the ring and, with a mighty heave, pulled open a trapdoor. Tiny winged Rahi and swarms of insects flew up, followed by a wave of damp, foul-smelling air.

"Not very pleasant, I will agree, but it is a shortcut," Whenua said with a shrug. "According to Nuparu, the damage is in the maintenance tunnels. The nickname for them is 'Fikou web,' after what the spiders leave down below, because the tunnels crisscross and twist around each other so."

"What if one of us gets lost?" asked Nokama.

"Don't," replied Whenua. "Just . . . don't. You wouldn't like it. The Matoran tell stories about repair crews that have been wandering down there since the early days of the Archives, unable to find their way out. They are supposed to have gone a little crazy. But, of course, those are just stories."

None of the Toa looked especially comforted by this. Matau had finally finished his tale and came over carrying six lightstones. "Just in case it is night-dark down there."

"Can I come?" asked Nuparu. "I can lead you right to the leak."

"You've done enough already," said Whenua. "I want you to go warn the archivists about this. Tell them we are going to do our best to fix the damage, but they should prepare to move exhibits out of the sub-basements in case they flood. Understand?"

Nuparu nodded and ran off. He understood why Whenua did not want him to come along, but it still frustrated him. As he rushed to carry out the Toa's instructions, he made a vow that someday he would invent something that would help Matoran better defend their homes from danger.

Whenua turned back to his friends, saying, "Hopefully, this won't take long. But be careful. There are always surprises in the Archives."

One by one, the Toa followed him down into the shaft. Only Matau seemed to hesitate, prompting Nokama to turn back and say, "What's the matter?"

"I do not like the below-ground," answered the Toa of Air. "I am a wind-flyer. Toa-hero adventures should only be on the surface, don't you think?"

"We can only hope," said Nokama as she vanished into the darkness.

The maintenance tunnels were to the underground what chutes were to the rest of Metru Nui: a quick means of transport from one end of the city to the other. Unlike chutes, which served everyone in Metru Nui, the tunnels were open only to those with authorization, normally Ta-Matoran and Onu-Matoran. Pipes big and small lined the walls of the tunnels, funneling liquid protodermis from place to place and molten protodermis to those locations that required extra heat.

Ordinarily, Matoran traveled through these tunnels by cart. But Matoran carts were too small for Toa Metru. Whenua idly wondered if the Toa should see about getting vehicles made for them in the future. Might save a lot of walking, swinging, and climbing.

The Toa of Earth felt uneasy. He knew the other Toa Metru were expecting him to take the lead on this mission, but his knowledge of the Fikou web was based largely on stories he had heard. He had never had cause to go much farther than the very outer edges of the tunnel network, and even that was with reluctance.

He was still worrying over this when he felt a cold breeze rush past him. It had come from deep in the maze, which made no sense — there should have been no openings to the outside up ahead. The only hatchways led up to the Archives, and certainly no breeze could come from there.

None of the other Toa seemed particularly disturbed by the strange wind or the drop in temperature. Whenua guessed they just didn't grasp the strangeness of the situation. He suddenly felt as if he could not take another step forward. Something was waiting up ahead, something far worse than any crack in the seawall, and they were walking right into its jaws. He just knew it.

His suspicions were confirmed a few moments later when a thick fog sprang from nowhere to engulf the Toa. Even their lightstones were of little use in penetrating the cloud. Whenua turned to find he could not make out any of his companions.

"Vakama? Nuju? Are you there?" he called out.

"Yes. What is this?" Vakama replied.

"I have never seen fog like this, not even in Ga-Metru," Nokama's voice added. "It is unnatural."

Just how unnatural it was became painfully obvious. A sudden flash of light almost blinded the Toa. An instant later, an impact sent Whenua crashing into his friends. Barely clinging to consciousness, the Toa of Earth said, "What in the name of Mata Nui was that?"

"A lightning bolt," answered Onewa. "A lightning bolt in an enclosed tunnel underground.

Is this normal in Onu-Metru, or are we just lucky?"

As if the freak storm had heard him, a second bolt flew toward the Toa of Stone. Acting on reflex, Onewa dove to the side as the bolt struck the wall where he had been.

"That was no accident," said Nokama. "Perhaps it's time we turned back and planned a strategy."

Nuju's voice broke through the fog. "If we could see where we are going, I would agree. As it is, I don't think we should turn our backs on an angry thundercloud."

"Quiet!" said Vakama. "Listen!"

The Toa Metru went silent. Now the air was filled with an ominous buzzing sound, which drew closer and closer. Not being able to see what caused it made it all the more frightening. "All right, keep calm," said Vakama. "Remember that we are Toa Metru, and we are together. As long as we stay united, we can overcome anything."

Privately, Vakama was not feeling quite so

confident. He thought he recognized that sound. If he was right, it came from a breed of Ta-Metru winged insects, nicknamed "fireflyers." Left alone, the small insects were relatively harmless. But when a swarm was angered, they would pursue an enemy halfway across the city.

Behind him, Matau had finally had enough. Bad enough to be wandering underground without all this danger and confusion. He raised his aero slicers and summoned a wind to blow the fog away. Although the best his weakened powers could manage was a stiff breeze, it was still enough to get the job done.

The fog dissipated, to reveal a sight out of every Matoran's nightmare: two powerful, menacing creatures, reptilianlike heads darting back and forth, staffs held tightly in their claws.

"Rahkshi!" shouted Whenua.

One of the Rahkshi was gold in color and now it screeched at the Toa. This Rahkshi had the ability to manipulate the weather within a limited range. Its partner, bright orange in color, was surrounded by a swarm of fireflyers. Controlled by the Rahkshi, the insects were just waiting for the signal to charge.

"What are they doing here?" asked Nokama.

"A better question is, what are we doing here?" said Onewa. "It took three squads of Vahki Zadakh to stop one Rahkshi that appeared in Po-Metru, and even then all they could do was drive the thing away."

"Then we will have to do better," said Nuju, blasting ice out of his crystal spikes. But his powers were not what they had been before the clash with the Morbuzakh, and the Rahkshi shrugged off the cold. The gold one hissed and unleashed a blizzard in the direction of the Toa.

Battered by wind and ice, the heroes fell back. Only Vakama saw the advantage they had gained — the intense cold was felling the firefly-ers one by one. Angered, the orange Rahkshi was now advancing on the gold one.

Now the Toa were witness to a scene of complete chaos. The gold Rahkshi had summoned another storm and was hurling lightning bolt after lightning bolt at its insect-controlling cousin. What it did not realize was that a swarm of tiny devourers was pouring forth from every crack in the walls and floors. Devourers would consume any bit of inorganic protodermis they ran across. Rahkshi armor was definitely on their menu — and all of them were hungry.

"This would be really entertaining if we didn't have to get past them to go on," said Onewa. "Whenua, you're the librarian, what do you know about these things?"

The Toa of Earth had by now shaken off the lightning strike and regained his feet. "Rahkshi are very territorial and quick to anger. If we make a move toward them, they'll forget their own fight and turn on us again."

"But this isn't about us, is it?" said Nokama. "They have claimed this portion of tunnel as their own and they are defending it."

"Then that is the answer," said Nuju. "We make it not worth the effort to defend. Vakama, Whenua, I will need your help."

Nuju outlined his plan in as few words as possible. The Rahkshi's clash was becoming even wilder, threatening to bring the tunnel down around them. When the Toa of Ice nodded his head, Vakama placed his palms on the floor and sent waves of scorching heat through the stone. Meanwhile, Nuju used the remains of his elemental power to create icicles on the roof of the tunnel.

Just as the Rahkshi took notice of the heat underfoot, Whenua went to work with his earthshock drills. Driving them into the ground, he formed a crevasse that ran straight toward the Rahkshi. Both of the creatures had figured out the Toa were somehow responsible for the sudden change in conditions, and they were not happy about it.

Nuju's plan had worked halfway. The Rahkshi were definitely uncomfortable, but not rattled enough to flee from their chosen home. Vakama loaded a disk in his launcher and hurled it through the air at the gold Rahkshi. When it struck, the enlarging power invested in the disk caused the Rahkshi to shoot up rapidly, smashing its head into the ceiling and bringing icicles raining down.

The insect-controlling Rahkshi did not react as Vakama hoped. Instead of fleeing into the darkness of the tunnels, it charged forward toward the Toa. Nokama and Vakama reacted as one, he launching fire and she water at the oncoming creature. But when their energy streams collided, the result was a wall of steam. By the time the cloud cleared away, the Rahkshi was nowhere to be seen.

"Somehow I don't think a steam bath frightened it away," said Nuju. "It will be back."

"Mata Nui! Why don't you watch what you're doing?" Nokama snapped at the Toa of Fire. "I might have stopped it if you hadn't gotten in the way."

"I got in the way? That wasn't how it looked from here."

Nokama was about to say something else when she changed her mind. Arguing wasn't going to make anything better. "I'm sorry, Vakama. Neither of us was at fault. But this is exactly why I have been saying we need leadership. We cannot keep blundering through challenges without any strategy."

"Here's a strategy," said Onewa. "Let's stop talking and start moving, before we get any more surprises."

The Toa Metru resumed their journey into the tunnels. None of them noticed another pair of eyes watching them, eyes far more observant than any Rahkshi's could be. They noted the way each Toa moved and fought, filing the information away for later use. Then the owner of those eyes slipped away into the darkness without making a sound.

The hunt had begun.

The Toa Metru did not encounter any more difficulties as they penetrated the outer edges of the maintenance tunnels. Now and then a small Rahi would skitter across their path, only to vanish down a hole or among the pipes. As they moved deeper into the maze, the air grew increasingly stale. Matau wondered aloud how Onu-Matoran could stand to work down here.

"Practice," said Whenua. "Most Onu-Matoran start out as miners, digging for lightstones. You get used to the dark pretty quickly. If you're lucky, you get the opportunity to become an archivist, but even then you are indoors and underground much of the time. These tunnels might be a little extreme, but nothing an Onu-Matoran can't handle."

Onewa looked around. "I don't see any Matoran though."

"Well . . . see . . . some of the ones who have come down here in the past sort of . . . haven't come back."

"You said that was a legend," said Nokama.

"Evidently, Onu-Matoran legend has a basis in fact," muttered Nuju.

"Anything else you forgot to tell us, Whenua?" asked Onewa.

Whenua raised his lightstone to give the Toa Metru a good look at what lay ahead. "Just that."

The wide tunnel they were walking through came to an abrupt end at a stone wall a few paces away. Six narrow openings were visible in the wall, barely more than slits in the rock. "This is the start of the Fikou web," said Whenua. "From here, it's just narrow tunnels drilled into the rock, crisscrossing with each other, until we reach the main tunnel on the other side."

"Do we split up?" asked Vakama.

Whenua nodded. "The major crack in the seawall is on the other side of the web, but there could be damage closer to us as well. Each of us should take a tunnel. We'll see each other as we go, I'm sure, and then we can all meet up on the other side. Hang on to your lightstones. If you lose them, you might become a permanent resident down here."

"That's what I like about Onu-Matoran," said Matau. "They are always so full of happy-cheer."

Nokama chose the left-most tunnel. The passage was so narrow that it would have been impossible for two Toa to walk abreast. For one used to the freedom of the protodermis canals and the open sea, this space was far too cramped to be comfortable. She could well believe Matoran could go mad from too much time down here.

Not for the first time, she wondered if becoming a Toa Metru had been such a good thing. So far, she did not seem to get along very well with any of her comrades. They were certainly not the five she would have chosen as companions. Only Vakama had struck her as possessing real wisdom behind his shy front, and now she had fought with him, too. She knew he had it in him to be a leader. Why wouldn't he recognize it?

Nokama forced herself to get back to the job at hand. Using the lightstone, she examined every bit of the walls on either side, looking for cracks or leaks. One of these tunnels could flood in an instant, and while she could probably survive that, she wasn't so sure about the other Toa Metru. She hoped they were being careful.

The tunnel wound around and around like the body of a serpent. Smaller passages broke off to the left and right, usually dead-ending rapidly. Still, each of them had to be examined. She wondered how Whenua could even have considered doing this job on his own — it would have taken forever!

After a while, Nokama started to grow bored. One tunnel looked just like the other, and none of them showed any signs of damage. She wondered if this might be just a wild Rahi chase. Some Matoran thought he saw something, panicked, and ran for the nearest Toa. Back when she was teaching in Ga-Metru, she made a point of telling her students to always make sure of their facts before they spread a tale.

She rounded a corner, expecting to see the same dull stone walls she had seen a hundred times before. Instead, she froze at the sight of the orange Rahkshi standing in the middle of the corridor. Its armored head was open, but no sound came from the creature.

Nokama readied her hydro blades. The Rahkshi simply stared at her. Neither seemed to want to make the first move.

The Toa of Water considered her options. If she advanced, she would surely have to challenge the Rahkshi and might or might not win. If she retreated, the Rahkshi might see it as a sign of weakness and pursue.

While Nokama was making up her mind, the Rahkshi raised its staff and pointed it at her. A swarm of fireflyers appeared from the darkness and flew straight for her. Even as she braced for their stings, Nokama wondered why the

Rahkshi looked so surprised at the display of its own power. The creature was actually backing away, as if afraid of what it had unleashed.

Not that its sudden show of regret did anything to help the Toa of Water. The insects were already swarming around her, stinging and then flying away, only to return and sting again. Nokama's armored body was enough to blunt most of their stings, but enough got through to drive her to the ground. As soon as she was subdued, the fireflyers left, their orders fulfilled.

Only the Rahkshi remained, standing over the unconscious form of a Toa.

In another tunnel, Vakama was wrestling with his thoughts. Despite some of the things she had said, he felt sure Nokama was truly his friend. She even seemed to think he should be the leader of the Toa Metru. True, he had done a decent job at that during the confrontation with the Morbuzakh, but he wasn't at all sure he would want the role permanently.

I might look like a Toa . . . even act like one

sometimes . . . but at heart, I am still a mask-maker, he said to himself. His whole life had been spent working alone at his forge, crafting protodermis into Matoran masks and Masks of Power. It required patience, skill, and dedication, but it did not seem like the ideal job to prepare someone to lead Toa.

This has all happened too fast, he thought. *I went from being an average Matoran to suddenly having all these new powers and responsibilities. Others look at me differently, expect more from me.*

He paused to shine his lightstone on the wall. The rock was unmarred by any crack and looked like it had not changed in an eternity. *So why did I have to change?* he wondered. *Am I still Vakama? Or am I only the Toa of Fire now?*

He walked on, lost in thought. His eyes inspected the tunnel as he traveled, but his mind was back in Ta-Metru. For a moment, he wondered if it would ever be possible to go back to being a Matoran. But no, the legends said nothing about such a thing. A Toa was a Toa until he fulfilled his destiny, and then . . . what?

So caught up was he in his questions that at first he did not hear the footsteps ahead of him. When he finally did, he stopped . . . and so did they. When he resumed walking, the footsteps started again. Vakama wanted to call out and see if it was another Toa Metru, but then realized it might be a Rahkshi instead. No point in giving away his position if it wasn't necessary.

He moved forward cautiously. The Toa had been caught by surprise a few times too often since their transformation. He was determined that it would not happen again.

Disk launcher primed and ready, Vakama took a deep breath and charged around the bend in the tunnel. Yes, there was a figure up ahead. Lean, powerful, carrying some kind of wickedly sharp tools, it moved silently through the shadows. Then it stepped out into the light to reveal —

"Nokama?" Vakama looked at the Toa of Water, stunned. They had just parted a short time ago. Had her tunnel crisscrossed with his so quickly? "Have you spotted anything, or not?"

The Toa of Water shook her head slowly. "Not."

Vakama moved closer to her, only to see Nokama step back. "What's the matter? It's just me. No reason for you to be afraid."

"Not afraid," Nokama replied. "Have you spotted anything?"

"Well, some little Rahi, some cart tracks, and a few Matoran names scrawled on the walls," said Vakama. "Nothing I would worry about."

"Matoran," Nokama repeated quietly, almost as if it were a curse. "Well, I would worry."

Vakama walked up to Nokama. She looked troubled. "What is it? Did you —?"

The Toa of Fire stopped in mid-sentence. He was having another one of his visions, sudden flashes of the future like the one that had warned him about the Morbuzakh. He saw Toa Onewa lying on the ground, unconscious, and standing over him was . . . Vakama!

A blast of water shattered the vision into a thousand pieces as the Toa of Fire went flying down the tunnel. He crashed hard into the stone wall and hit the floor. Before he could gather his wits and get up again, Nokama had him pinned with the force of her water bursts. Even as his body struggled to get free, his mind struggled with questions. Why was she doing this? How had her elemental energies been restored to full power? Was Nokama planning to betray the other Toa Metru, and if so, for what purpose?

Vakama hoped to ask the Toa of Water these questions, if he was ever able to take another breath. But driven to the ground by the sheer, raw power of twin jets of water, it seemed more likely that he was about to become the first Toa to ever drown on dry land.

The gold Rahkshi moved carefully down the tunnel. Every one of its senses was on the alert. There were still intruders in its territory, and that was very bad. Intruders made loud noises and tried to drive the Rahkshi away, unless the Rahkshi struck first.

It could not hear the six from before, but it could smell them. They were no longer together and their scent carried traces of fear. That was pleasing to the Rahkshi. When the ones from up above carried fear into the tunnels, they were easier to find and easier to drive off.

The Rahkshi tried hard to remember how it had come to live in this place. But it could not. It had a vague memory of once living someplace else, then a long journey to the land above. But there were too many others there who tried to capture it. The Rahkshi escaped and fled down, down into the cold, welcoming dark.

The creature paused as it sensed another presence up ahead. Another Rahkshi, but not a threat. It stayed close to the wall as it moved forward until the other came into view. It was the orange Rahkshi from before, but now it was stretched out on the ground and not moving.

The gold Rahkshi crept closer. Why was the other so still? Was it hurt? Had the cold sleep overtaken it? No, the wormlike kraata inside was only stunned. Still, it wondered what could strike down a Rahkshi like this. Not one of the little ones from above. Not one of the six.

Wait! There was a scent in the air, strong and not unfamiliar to the Rahkshi. It had encountered a creature before with this scent, long ago when it first came to the tunnels. It sifted through dim memories trying to bring the image of the creature into focus.

Then suddenly the Rahkshi remembered it all. And with the memory came something else, something none of its kind had ever felt before . . .

Fear.

Onewa pulled himself painfully up to his hands and knees. He wasn't sure how long the world had been black, or exactly how he had wound up on the tunnel floor, unconscious.

The sight of scorch marks on the stone wall started bringing it all back to him. He had been exploring the tunnel when someone came up behind him. It was Vakama. The Toa of Fire seemed distracted, but he agreed to help Onewa check out some of the side passages. The Toa of Stone went back to work and then . . .

He did it! Onewa realized. *I felt the heat, and then the next thing I knew stalactites were falling down all around me.*

The Toa of Stone glanced up, already knowing what he would see. The stalactites had not broken off naturally — well-placed fire bursts had melted them free from the ceiling.

Onewa didn't know why a fellow Toa Metru would try to harm him, and he didn't really care. All that mattered was finding Vakama and showing him just what stone could do against fire.

In another tunnel not far away, Nokama too was awakening. She still ached from the fireflyer stings, but it was nothing she couldn't survive. No, she had something far more important to worry about.

In her mind, she went over every detail of her encounter with the insect-controlling Rahkshi. She recalled its every movement, its reaction to her, even the way its armored head had opened to allow the kraata inside to screech.

But it never made a sound, she realized. *When the armored plates opened . . . there was no kraata inside!*

Nokama was no Rahkshi expert. She had seen them in stasis tubes in the Archives, like any other Matoran, and one of them had run amok once in Ga-Metru before the Vahki brought it down. But she knew enough to be certain that a Rahkshi without its kraata was just an empty, if still frightening, suit of armor.

So that wasn't a Rahkshi, she thought grimly. *Not unless they grow them differently down here. I'd almost think I had imagined the whole thing, but the stings are real. It was something that* looked *like a Rahkshi, had the powers of one, and . . .*

Once, a long time before, Nokama and some of her friends had been playing near the canals on the border of Ga-Metru and Ko-Metru. Nokama had slipped and fallen in. The current had swept her into the other metru. The liquid protodermis had turned frigid when it traveled through Ko-Metru, and by the time she was rescued, she was half frozen. But that chill was nothing compared to what ran through her now.

If it can look like a Rahkshi, what else can it look like? she asked herself, already breaking into a run. *Or . . .* who *else?*

Vakama was furious.

He had awakened to find Nokama gone.

Apparently, the Toa of Water thought she had finished him off. He was on his way to prove her very wrong.

Toa Nuju had been walking for a very long time. At least, it seemed that way. As much as he disliked agreeing with Matau on anything, he was no more comfortable underground than was the Toa of Air. He missed the spires of Ko-Metru, the clean, crisp air, and most of all, the sight of the stars streaking by overhead. He belonged atop a Knowledge Tower, keeping watch over his metru, not wandering around Onu-Metru maintenance tunnels looking for leaks. Really, was this work for a Toa Metru?

Still, at least these narrow passages gave him an excuse to get away from the other Toa. If he had to listen to more arguing, or another one of Matau's bad jokes, he was going to freeze the whole lot of them. Maybe after they presented themselves to Turaga Dume at the Coliseum, he could go his own way and simply be the Toa of Ko-Metru.

His planning for the future was interrupted by a tremor that shook the entire tunnel network. This was followed by what sounded like a rock slide not far ahead. Images of the whole place coming down and trapping the six Toa Metru flashed through his mind. Nuju raced ahead, hoping he was wrong about what he had heard.

It was almost worse than he had expected. A whole portion of one of the walls had collapsed, and the glow from the lightstone revealed Matau half buried in stone. Nuju tried to freeze the rocks, with the idea of shattering them once frozen, but his power was too weak. Instead, he had to remove them one by one as he dug out the Toa of Air.

Matau revived just as Nuju finished. His eyes sparked to life and he hurled a mini-cyclone at Nuju. The Toa of Ice was blown back, but not hard enough to injure himself. "What was that for?" he demanded.

"Nuju? Is that you?" asked Matau.

"How many Toa of Ice do you think are

walking around down here?" Nuju said, giving Matau a hand up. "What happened to you?"

"Onewa," said Matau. "He's mad-crazy. I said hello and he brought the wall down on me."

"That doesn't sound like him," Nuju said, frowning. "You, maybe, but not him. Did you say anything to anger Onewa?"

Matau shook his head. "No. He waved and slide-down came the rocks. And look at this!"

The Toa of Air pointed to a spot high on the partially ruined wall. Nuju leaned in close and saw it was a burn mark. "He did that, too," insisted Matau. "Whoosh, hot-flame."

"All right. We had better find him," Nuju replied. "Before he finds someone else."

Nokama raced through the tunnels, fighting down her panic. A Rahkshi that wasn't a Rahkshi . . . what if Nuparu had not been Nuparu? What if all of this was an elaborate trap for the Toa Metru? Bring them down into the dark, separate them, and then . . .

No, she told herself. *Get ahold of yourself. Of course, Nuparu was really who he seemed to be. The crisis down here is real, but so is the danger if I don't find the other Toa Metru soon.*

Nokama's wish was granted in the next moment, as a fireball whizzed past her. It was too far away to be meant as anything but a warning, but it still made her ready her hydro blades. Her eyes struggled to pierce the darkness to find the source of the flame.

"This time you don't catch me by surprise." Vakama walked out of the shadows, disk launcher raised. "I don't know why you chose to turn on us, Nokama, but you'll never win."

"Wait! You don't understand!" Nokama shouted.

"You should have made sure I was defeated, Nokama," the Toa of Fire said as he launched a Kanoka disk at the Toa of Water.

Nokama didn't hesitate. She dove aside as the disk narrowly missed her. An instant later, it struck a stalagmite and shrunk it down to the size of a pebble. Nokama gasped.

"Vakama, don't make me defend myself," she cried. "Please listen to me!"

"I'll be glad to, once I know you're wrapped up tight," the Toa of Fire answered. He bent down and placed his palm on the stone floor. Nokama's eyes widened as the rock began to glow red, the wave of heat heading right for her.

"That . . . does . . . it!" Nokama said, launching herself into a flip. In midair, she hurled blasts of water at Vakama. Caught unawares, the Toa of Fire was swept off his feet and hit the ground hard. Nokama twisted her body and landed behind him.

But Vakama was ready for her. Guessing correctly where she would land, he rolled and came up launching another disk. This one found its target and Nokama felt an awful weakness overtake her. She dropped to her knees, barely able to hold her tools aloft.

The Toa of Fire got to his feet. "Stay down, Nokama. Please."

Nokama lifted her head and looked at Vakama. A horrible thought struck her: How could she know if this was really her friend? Maybe whatever impersonated the Rahkshi was after her again, this time in the form of someone she trusted. If that was the case, she couldn't afford to lose this struggle. Who knew what this . . . whatever it was . . . might be planning for the other Toa Metru?

Nokama struggled to draw on her elemental energies. If she could flood the tunnel, she could escape and warn the others. But she moved too slowly. Vakama had another disk ready, and was about to launch.

A sudden tremor rocked the tunnel. Rock rained down on the Toa of Fire, knocking him to the ground. Nokama looked past him to see the source: Onewa, eyes gleaming, proto pitons driven into the ground.

"Get away from her, Vakama," he snarled. "Time to put out your fire."

Nuju and Matau felt the tremor and immediately quickened their pace. "Do you have a thought-plan on what we do if Onewa's really turned bad?"

"We stop him," Nuju replied.

"No wonder you were a quick-smart scholar," Matau said, making no attempt to hide his sarcasm. "Then what? Give him to the Vahki? How will that make the rest of us Toa-heroes look?"

Matau had a good point. Nuju hated it when that happened. He could just picture showing up at the Coliseum to meet Turaga Dume, five Toa Metru with one tied up for delivery to the order enforcement squads. What kind of confidence would that inspire in the Matoran of Metru Nui? They would be finished before they even got started.

Another tremor shook the tunnels. "Let's worry about that when we capture him," said Nuju. "If we capture him."

Vakama was in the middle of a nightmare.

On one side, Nokama had recovered from her bout of weakness and was sending spheres of water in his direction. On the other, Onewa, apparently infected with the same madness she was, was bringing down half the tunnel. All the while, the Toa of Stone was ranting some nonsense about Vakama ambushing him.

Vakama still had no idea what was wrong with the two of them, but one thing was certain, he could not defeat two Toa Metru. It was all he could do to dodge Nokama's powers while melting the stone Onewa rained down on him. He wondered where Nuju, Matau, and Whenua were, or whether they had already fallen to their traitorous "friends."

There was no way Vakama could keep dodging forever without making a mistake. Moving to avoid flying rock, he placed himself in the path of one of Nokama's water bursts. The impact sent him to his knees. Onewa moved in for the capture.

"Maybe Turaga Dume will know how to heal whatever's wrong with you, fire-spitter," said the Toa of Stone. "Now I'll take the disk launcher."

Onewa reached for Vakama's Toa tool. But before he could grab it away, a sudden gust of wind lifted the Toa of Stone off his feet and hurled him down the tunnel. Vakama looked up to see Matau and Nuju standing nearby.

"Surprise," said the Toa of Air. "We followed your earth-shakers, Onewa, and got here everquick. Now why did you drop a wall on me?"

So I was right, Vakama thought. *Something* is *wrong with Onewa. Matau just proved it!*

Nokama rushed to help Onewa up and the two of them stood together. "You're wrong,

Matau. It's Vakama that has turned bad, not Onewa. You have to help us stop him."

"No! Onewa has tricked you," answered Matau.

"Something is very wrong here," Nuju said, just loud enough to catch everyone's attention. "Vakama took me by surprise, and Nokama says he did Onewa, too. But Matau says Onewa is the culprit . . . an Onewa who has the power of fire as well as stone."

"That's crazy!" snapped Onewa. "I haven't even seen Matau since we split up!"

"And Nokama challenged me," said Vakama. "This place must be driving us all mad."

"I suggest we stop fighting until we figure out the truth," said Nuju.

Slowly, reluctantly, the other Toa Metru accepted the wisdom of his words. They lowered their Toa tools and eyed one another warily. Onewa and Nokama stood on one side, Nuju and Matau on the other, and Vakama in the middle. But the voice that finally broke the uncomfortable silence did not belong to any of the five of them.

"About time," said Whenua, walking down the tunnel. "I thought I was going to have to wade into the middle of all of you."

The other Toa Metru all began talking at once, either warning Whenua or trying to explain how the conflict started. It was impossible to make out anything in the chaos of voices.

"Enough!" Whenua shouted. "You're all wrong. All of you were ambushed by another Toa Metru . . . and none of you were."

"What are you talking about?" demanded Onewa. "I know what happened to me."

Only Nokama seemed to understand. "Of course . . . the Rahkshi I saw —"

"Let me guess," said Whenua. "It looked like a Rahkshi, but something was off."

"Yes! How did you know?"

"It's called a Krahka, and I encountered it, too," the Toa of Earth explained. "A very dangerous Rahi. She defends herself by mimicking the appearance of an enemy, so well that she adapts their powers and abilities, too."

"That explains 'Onewa' using stone and fire powers at once. This Krahka must have adapted Vakama's powers and then his," said Nuju.

"But why is she after us? What did we do?" asked Nokama.

Whenua frowned. "This is her territory. We're intruders. Maybe she wants to drive us out."

"So what do we do? Run back up to Metru Nui because this thing wants us to?" said Onewa. "What about the Archives? What about the flooding?"

Whenua didn't have an answer for that. It was Vakama who finally said, "We stick together from now on. That way we can't be taken by surprise."

"That's quick-smart," said Matau. "And maybe we should hunt-track this Krahka before we worry about the leak."

"No!" said Whenua. "I think we need to get out now. You don't know what a Krahka is capable of."

The Toa Metru looked at one another. It

was Whenua's metru, and they had planned on letting him take the lead. But Toa running from anything, for any reason, felt wrong. Nuju put their feelings into words, saying, "Are we going to the Coliseum, then — or fleeing to it?"

Nokama looked at Vakama, thinking, *This is the time. Step up and be a leader. Make this decision.*

But Vakama didn't speak. Instead, it was Onewa who said, "No mindless Rahi is going to make me run. I say we go on, capture this thing, and then do what we set out to do here. Who's with me?"

One by one, all of the Toa Metru stepped forward. Whenua was the last to join the group. "All right, if we are going to do this," the Toa of Earth said, "then I better act as guide. I can take a guess where the Krahka might be hiding."

The six Toa Metru started walking through the tunnels, Whenua in the lead. Matau and Nuju trailed along behind, the Toa of Air looking puzzled.

"Nuju?"

"What?"

"If this Krahka can seem-look like anything it's seen . . . how will we know when we have found it?"

It was a very good question. Nuju wished he had a very good answer.

They had not been traveling for very long before most of the Toa Metru lost all track of where they were or how to get back. No one had thought to mark a trail as they proceeded through the tunnels. For his part, Whenua moved through the maze with complete confidence, never hesitating at any of the intersections.

So far, the journey had been without incident. The few small Rahi they had encountered ran from them. At one point, Vakama thought he spotted the gold Rahkshi, but it disappeared into the shadows before he could get a good look.

"Elementary translation," Nokama said softly.

Nuju turned to her. "What?"

"Elementary translation. That's what I would have been teaching today . . . if I had not become a Toa Metru."

"Do you regret the change?" asked the Toa of Ice.

Nokama shrugged. "No. No, of course not. We are heroes, aren't we? We can do things no one else can. But . . . when was the last time you saw a Toa playing a sport? Or jumping into chutes for the fun of it? Or doing any of the things Matoran do every day?"

Silence was Nuju's answer. His memory of Toa Lhikan was of a larger than life figure, defending the city against any threat and then returning, exhausted, to wait for the next call to action. He never seemed to have time for fun or friendship.

"I am not complaining about all we have gained," Nokama continued. "Just missing all we may have lost."

"Perhaps it is up to us to be a different kind of Toa Metru," said Nuju. "And to make sure that any Toa who follow us learn these lessons as well."

Whenua held up a hand. "Stop. Look ahead."

The floor of the tunnel before them had

collapsed, evidently long ago. A flimsy bridge made from Le-Metru cable had been constructed over the chasm. It was the right width and strength for a party of Matoran crossing, but looked far too weak to support six Toa Metru.

"Is there another way across?" asked Nokama.

Whenua shook his head.

"Then we go this way, earth-digger," said Onewa. "One at a time."

The bridge consisted of a single cable, attached to two others higher up that served as handrails. Whenua stepped carefully onto the cable and began to quickly make his way across. When he was halfway across the span, the darkness below the bridge began to move.

"Mata Nui protect us . . . what is that?" said Nokama.

Nuju peered over the edge. "Stone rats. Thousands of them."

"Hundreds of thousands," said Vakama. "Their warrens must have been disturbed when the tunnel collapsed."

"Dangerous?" asked Matau.

"You wouldn't want one for a pet," Onewa replied. "Their teeth are made for eating through solid rock. Put an Ussal cart or a chute, or even a Knowledge Tower, between them and dinner and they'll eat that, too."

Whenua kept moving as if he hadn't even noticed the creatures below. He reached the other side and beckoned the others to follow. Nokama took a step onto the bridge and paused, seeing the thousands of red eyes down below and hearing the chittering of hungry stone rats.

"How come the Chronicles never talk about things like this?" she said.

"Probably because the Chronicler ran away," Onewa chuckled. "Only Toa are brave enough for this kind of work."

"Brave enough, or foolish enough?"

"Brave, if we make it across," the Toa of Stone answered. "Foolish, if we don't."

Nokama closed her eyes and focused all her concentration within. Ga-Metru Matoran were trained in both mental and physical disciplines, for the two went hand in hand. She struggled to remember all that she had learned about maintaining perfect balance. When she finally felt ready, the Toa of Water opened her eyes and started across the bridge.

As she walked, slowly and steadily, nothing existed for her except the cable beneath her feet. There were no rats below, no Toa behind, no sights or sounds that were not directly related to her task. She was not even aware that she had made it to the other side until Whenua grabbed her hand to steady her for the last few steps.

"Well, if she can do it . . ." said Matau. Then he sprang into the air, flipped over, and grabbed both hand cables. As the other Toa watched in shock, he proceeded to cross the bridge by walking on his hands. "This is the way a Toa-hero does it!"

"That's the way an Ussal driver who's gone round one chute too many does it," muttered Onewa. "Vakama, you're next."

If the Toa of Fire was fearful, he didn't show it. Disk launcher at the ready, he walked as swiftly as he could across the cable. He had almost reached the end when he heard Nokama shout his name.

Vakama whirled to see a ghostly figure rising from out the sea of stone rats. At first its identity wasn't clear. But as it passed through the bridge to hover in the air, he could see it was a Rahkshi with a black head and spine, and dark green claws and feet. Vakama launched a disk at the floating creature, only to see it pass right through the target.

"Nothing to fear-worry about," said Matau. "If you can't touch it, then it can't touch you, right?"

The Rahkshi screeched in answer. Then before the Toa's startled eyes, it went from ghostly to solid and plunged down. The creature struck the bridge, tearing one end loose. Vakama grabbed the cable and hung on as he slammed into the rock wall.

Down below, the stone rats scrambled in anticipation of the Rahkshi falling toward them. At the last moment, the creature's density changed once more and it floated upward again.

Frustrated, a few of the stone rats turned to the end of the cable bridge now resting in their midst. Cautiously at first, they began to climb the cable. Seeing their success, more began to follow, crawling toward Vakama.

The Toa of Fire climbed hand over hand toward the ledge. Nokama held out her hydro blade for him to grab on to. "Hurry! They're coming!"

Vakama looked down. The stone rats were now racing up the cable. In moments, they would be upon him and then up onto the ledge where Nokama, Matau, and Whenua stood. He could tell he would not make it all the way up in time. There was only one thing left to do.

Grabbing a disk, Vakama slammed it into the cable. The weakness power in the Kanoka disk combined with the sharp edge of the disk itself to sever the line. Toa of Fire, bridge, and stone rats fell together toward the chasm far below.

"Vakama!" Nokama screamed.

Onewa and Nuju watched helplessly as their friend plummeted down. "Ice?"

"I tried," said Nuju. "My elemental powers are exhausted!"

Matau pushed past Nokama. "Not losing a Toa-friend today!" Before she could stop him, he dove off the ledge.

Vakama saw the Toa of Air plunging toward him. Matau was shouting, "Slow yourself! Flip over, Vakama!"

The Toa of Fire had no idea what Matau was planning, but he wasn't going to argue. Letting go of the cable, Vakama executed a series of midair flips to slow his fall. As he completed the third one, he felt Matau grab his wrists.

"Now we go high-flying!" shouted Matau.

A sudden gust of wind lifted both Toa toward the ceiling. Vakama glanced below to see the cable bridge disappearing beneath the swarm of stone rats.

"Beats ground-walking now, doesn't it?" laughed Matau.

"Sure. Unless you fly right into a Rahkshi. Watch out!"

Matau turned to see the Rahkshi hovering right in his path. Unable to shift the winds in time to change their course, he and Vakama plunged right through the misty substance of the creature. Then the Rahkshi suddenly solidified and grabbed on to Vakama's leg. Toa Metru and Rahkshi dropped like a stone.

"Matau! We need a stronger wind!" shouted Vakama.

"Or one less wind-rider!" snapped Matau.

The Toa of Fire tried to shake off the Rahkshi, but the creature wasn't letting go. He mustered the strongest flame he could, but the Rahkshi simply turned insubstantial and let the fire go right through it before resuming its grip on Vakama.

"It's not letting go!"

"It will, Toa-brother," replied Matau. "I don't think it will like where we're going!"

The Toa of Air summoned all his strength and channeled it into a powerful wind that flung the three of them on a collision course with the rock wall. Vakama glanced up to see complete determination in Matau's eyes. He never wavered as he steered them directly toward a final crash.

Great, thought Vakama. *Never thought my last moments would be spent with a deranged Toa who thinks he's a Gukko bird.*

The Toa of Fire was tempted to close his eyes as the wall grew closer and closer. But he did not. Toa Lhikan would have met his end with eyes open and head held high, and Vakama would not shame that tradition by showing fear.

An instant before a certain, shattering impact, Matau suddenly swerved upward, taking Vakama with him. The Rahkshi was whipped hard toward the wall and instinctively turned intangible to avoid the crash. Its hands slipped right through Vakama's ankle and it sailed off, passing through the rock and disappearing into the wall.

Matau winced at the sight. "Hope that Rahkshi doesn't think to go solid while it's in there."

Suddenly, the Toa dropped, rose, and then dropped again. "What's going on?" asked Vakama.

"My power is fading!" answered Matau. "The winds won't close-listen anymore!"

The Toa of Air fought to stay aloft. More than once, it looked as if they were going to become much better acquainted with the stone rats than either Toa wanted to. Finally, Matau managed to steer them above the ledge where Nokama and Whenua waited. That was when his power at last gave out completely, sending them both toward the stone floor.

Nokama moved quickly to catch Vakama. But Matau fell hard right in front of Whenua, who did not act in time to prevent it. "Thanks for the quick-save," the Toa of Air grumbled. "Next time, you can rescue the fire-spitter and I will stay safe on the ledge."

"What you did was very brave," Nokama said to Matau. "But you shouldn't have had to do it." She turned to Vakama. "We could have handled the stone rats, if it came to that, Vakama. You didn't have to sacrifice yourself."

There was no anger in her words, but they stung just the same. Worse, Vakama knew she was right. They were all Toa Metru now. By acting like he had to protect the others, he had only succeeded in placing his and Matau's lives at risk.

Will I ever be done learning how to be a Toa? he wondered. *The lessons keep getting harder. Fail one and you may not get a chance to try another.*

"I wish I could say all is well, but we still have a problem," said Nokama, gesturing across the chasm. "Make that three. Two Toa Metru on the other side, and no bridge. So . . . whose turn is it to come up with the great idea?"

Watching from the other side, Onewa shook his head. "If we wait for that group to save us, we will end up Rahi bones here. What do you say we take a leap into the future, Nuju?"

Before the Toa of Ice could respond, Onewa had grabbed him by the arm and jumped off the ledge. His powerful legs propelled them well out over the chasm, but nowhere near far enough to reach the other Toa. It looked as if the stone rats were about to receive two unexpected gifts.

Onewa did not look at all worried. As the

two Toa reached the apex of their leap, he used his Toa power on the ground far below. An instant later, a pillar of stone shot up midway across the span and directly in the path of the Toa of Stone.

Casting one of his proto pitons ahead of him, Onewa caught the pillar with it and swung to relative safety, Nuju in tow. The Toa of Ice looked at him and said coldly, "Don't . . . *ever* . . . do . . . that . . . again."

"Relax, scholar," replied Onewa. "You'll get used to it."

With a yell, Onewa launched the two of them into the air again. The other Toa Metru scattered just in time as they landed on the ledge, Onewa tucking and rolling to minimize the impact and Nuju crashing hard into the rock.

The Toa of Stone was the first to reach his feet, in time to see Nuju rise and charge toward him. Vakama moved quickly to keep the two apart. "If my powers were at their peak, hammer-swinger, no one would be hearing from you until the thaw," growled Nuju.

"Big talk from a stargazer," snapped Onewa. "Try doing real work sometime."

"Hold it!" said Vakama. "Both of you. We have done enough fighting among ourselves."

"This is no way for Toa Metru to behave," said Nokama. "What would Turaga Dume say if he saw this?"

"Turaga Dume will never get the chance to anger-speak or anything else to us if we don't get moving," said Matau. "Save the shout-loud for when we are out of this place."

"Yes, let us keep going. We are almost at the end," said Whenua, frowning. Without waiting for an answer from his friends, he turned and started walking farther into the tunnels.

Matau watched him go and shook his head. "If he gets any more dark and grim, I will call him Toa of Mud."

Nokama said nothing. But her eyes never left Whenua as the team resumed its journey.

The Toa of Stone caught up to Whenua sometime later. "Any plan for what we do when we find this thing?"

"No," Whenua answered.

"Ever had to get a shape-shifter like this into the Archives before?"

The Toa of Earth seemed to puzzle over that question for a long time, before he finally said, "How would we know if we had?"

The path narrowed, and then widened again. Although their lightstones were still working well, the gloom seemed heavier here and the shadows harder to drive away. Eventually, despite the bright glow of the stones, the darkness became impossible to pierce and the Toa Metru were forced to halt.

"This cannot be natural," said Nokama quietly. "This blackness feels almost . . . alive."

"I think you are imagining things," said Nuju. "Darkness is just the absence of light. It cannot be a living thing."

"Let's keep going," said Onewa. "Follow my voice, this way. No, wait, I think that's the way we came. Maybe we had better go the other way. I —"

The Toa of Stone's voice cut off abruptly. Nokama called his name, but he did not answer. The other Toa Metru stood perfectly still, but could not hear their friend — or anything else — moving.

Finally, Whenua said, "This way," and the others moved toward the sound. They walked single file, the Toa of Earth in the lead, followed by Nokama, Nuju, Matau, and Vakama. If Onewa was trailing along behind, he gave no sign. Every now and then, one of the Toa would glance over their shoulder, but no one could see anything through the shadows.

Vakama was troubled. Onewa might not be the easiest Toa to work with, but he was no coward. He wouldn't have just run off and abandoned his friends.

Something happened to him, and if we're not careful, the same thing will happen to us, he said to himself.

Even as the words raced through Vakama's mind, something snaked through the darkness to wrap around his legs, arms, and mask. For a moment, he thought perhaps the Morbuzakh vines had returned, but this felt different. Then lack of air cut off his thoughts and he blacked out. The mysterious thing that had grabbed Vakama now dragged him away.

"Vakama, perhaps your fire could brighten the way," Nokama said. "Do you have enough power left to try?"

But the Toa of Fire did not answer. Nokama stopped short, and Nuju walked into her. "Why are you stopping?" asked the Toa of Ice.

"I think Vakama is gone, too!" she answered. "Something is in this darkness with us, Nuju. How do we fight what we can't see?"

She reached out to find Nuju. But her hand

instead encountered what felt like an energy field. A tingle ran up her arm and she pulled back violently as her limb began to grow dead. "Nuju! I felt something!"

When Nokama extended her arm a second time, the field was gone . . . and so was the Toa of Ice.

"Whenua! Matau! Are you there?"

"Ground-walking right behind you," said Matau. "What's happened to the others?"

"They found side passages?" suggested Whenua.

Nokama was surprised that the Toa of Earth did not sound more concerned. But then he knew better than any of them how easy it was to get lost down here.

"I think we should link hands," Nokama said.

"Great idea!" Matau replied. "But maybe Whenua should scout ahead, and we two can stay hand-linked back here."

"Very funny, Matau."

Nokama took hold of Whenua's hand. But when she reached for Matau's, the Toa of Air was gone. It took every bit of her willpower not to panic. If the other Toa were in danger, only she and Whenua were left to save them.

Now Whenua was tugging her forward so hard that she almost left her feet. The darkness was breaking up around her now and she could see flashes of stone walls. The next moment, the oppressive shadow was gone completely and Nokama blinked as she adjusted to the sudden light.

She and Whenua were standing in a cavern, alone. There was no sign of the other Toa or what had taken them. The Toa of Earth looked around and said, "I warned them this would be dangerous. We should have turned back."

"It's too late for that now," snapped Nokama. "We have to find them. I'm not leaving these tunnels without the others."

"Well, that's half right," muttered Whenua. "Going back will just get us trapped. We should go forward. If they are lost . . . I doubt they will ever be found."

Nokama whirled to look at the Toa of Earth. Whenua had made those comments as if he were talking about a misplaced tool. "You're right, Whenua. It is very dangerous down here, isn't it? But the Toa of Earth volunteered to guide us through the tunnels of his metru. That way, we could avoid the most perilous spots — or could we?"

She crossed her hydro blades in front of her and took a step back, now battle ready. "The six Toa Metru could triumph over any foe. But if one of us was *not* one of us, treachery would win the day. That is what you counted on, wasn't it, Krahka?"

Before Nokama's eyes, "Whenua" morphed into the exact image of Vakama. "I wondered when you would figure it out, Toa. You would not leave my domain, even when one of your own suggested it . . . and now you will never leave."

"So some of what you said was the truth," Nokama answered. "You can look like any one of us. And you were the Rahkshi I encountered, weren't you?"

Another shift and now Nokama was facing the yellow Rahkshi. Then she turned back to

Vakama. "Yes. No real Rahkshi would be fooled, but their senses are more acute than yours."

"Why go to all this trouble?" Nokama said, circling to get the best defensive position. "Why not just appear as Turaga Dume and order us out of the tunnels?"

"I can only take the form of those I have encountered," said the Krahka, quickly shape-shifting from Vakama to Nuju to Onewa. "And it took me time to learn your language. When I first met Vakama, in your shape, I could only repeat back words he had said to me."

Now the Krahka cycled through all six Toa Metru, ending up as Whenua again. "Now I have learned. I have adapted. It is too late for all of you."

"Where's the real Whenua? What have you done to him?"

"No more than I did to the rest of the Toa," the Krahka said in Whenua's booming voice. "These tunnels are a haven for Rahkshi. Rahkshi who can coil their elastic bodies around you . . . or teleport you away . . . or trap you in a stasis field . . . or simply cloak you in silence so no one can hear you scream."

Nokama kept moving, staying out of reach of the Krahka. She knew that the longer the Rahi talked, the more time her elemental powers would have to strengthen. "Why not just let us leave? We mean no harm to you."

For just a split second, the Krahka took on the hideous form of a half Rahkshi, half Toa. Then she changed to Matau. "Because you would not leave. Top-dwellers never do. But this is my place. Here you are the invaders. You are not welcome."

Nokama started to reply, then stopped short. The Krahka's words could have just as easily been said by the Toa to the Morbuzakh plant when it threatened Metru Nui. Was this creature really doing nothing more than defending her home? Still, Nokama had to save her friends. If the Krahka was determined to get in the way, then a clash was inevitable.

"You realize if we don't return, more 'top-dwellers' will come down here," said the Toa of

Water. "They will search for us. Your home will be torn apart. Is that really what you want?"

"If they search for you, they will find you," said the Krahka, shifting to Vakama's form. Then in the voice of the Toa of Fire, she said, "The Toa Metru have discovered a danger to the city lurking far underground. We are going to stay here until the danger is ended."

Nokama's mind reeled. She had never even considered . . . but it made sense. The Krahka could fool everyone into thinking the Toa safe and on a mission. For that matter, other than Nuparu, who even knew they were down here? Who would go looking for them?

Three shapes emerged from the tunnels and into the cave. They were Rahkshi, one silver, one black-white, one tan-blue. "I sensed great power in you, Nokama, more than you realize," said the Krahka. "It is a shame you will never live up to your potential."

Vakama/Krahka slipped away as the three Rahkshi moved in. They seemed to shy away from the Krahka, perhaps disturbed by the conflict between what they scented and what they saw. But they had no such reluctance about pursuing Nokama.

The three spread out, surrounding Nokama. She feinted right and then dove for the legs of the tan-blue Rahkshi. But when she reached the spot, the creature faded away as if it had never been there. Then it reappeared a short distance away.

Teleportation? Nokama wondered as she scrambled to her feet. *No . . . illusion. I see it where it's not.*

She did not have much time to think about that. The silver Rahkshi hurled a lightning bolt in her direction. She managed to dodge the full impact, but enough of the energy brushed her that she was thrown across the room. Nokama never struck the ground, though. Instead, she found herself whirled about in a cyclone created by the black-white Rahkshi.

When the winds abruptly died down, Nokama landed hard on the cavern floor. Staggering, she had to make a real effort to draw herself up to her hands and knees. The three Rahkshi stood their ground, not coming close enough for her to grab. She tried to stand up, but a jagged bolt of lightning just above her head killed that idea.

Strangely enough, the Rahkshi's actions made her feel less fearful. If they had been convinced they could defeat her, they would have closed in already. Instead, they maintained their distance and tried to keep her off balance.

They don't know what to make of me, she realized. *Maybe they have never seen a Toa before. That means they have no idea how powerful I might be.*

"I appreciate the rest. All that walking was tiring," she said, trying to sound confident. "You do not believe a mere three of you can stop a Toa, though, do you?"

The Rahkshi stirred. They didn't understand the words, but they sensed that the tone was not that of a defeated foe. Nokama was trying to decide what to do next when she heard a welcome sound — the dripping of liquid protodermis through a minute crack in the wall. The leak was only a short distance away, to her left, but the black-white Rahkshi was between her and the slowly forming puddle.

Just where I want him, she thought.

"Compared to what I just faced up above, you three aren't even worth wasting my Toa power on. Oh, maybe you scare all the little Rahi that skitter around down here, but up above we laugh at things like you," she continued.

Nokama kept talking to distract the Rahkshi from what she was really doing — extending her power to draw a stream of liquid protodermis from the site of the leak right to her. Conveniently, the stream passed right beneath the feet of the black-white Rahkshi.

"Actually, you are fortunate to have run into me," she said, mockingly. "Vakama or Nuju, they might really hurt you."

The thin line of liquid had almost reached her. The black-white Rahkshi's attention was focused on her. It had never noticed what she had done. Now it was time to see if her plan was going to work.

She locked her gaze on the silver Rahkshi and snarled, "I have had enough of this. Get out of my way." Then she lunged forward as if about to spring.

The Rahkshi reacted with a bolt of chain lightning, but Nokama wasn't sitting and waiting for it. Instead of springing, she rolled to her left. The bolt struck where she had been, hitting the stream of protodermis and traveling along it right back to the black-white Rahkshi. The current slammed into the creature and sent him flying.

Nokama swung her hydro blades hard and cleaved open the wall at the site of the leak. Liquid protodermis gushed through the gap, rapidly filling the cave. Both Rahkshi's faceplates opened to reveal very disturbed kraata, screeching their rage.

Then she noticed an unexpected benefit of the flood. The liquid was disturbed a few feet to the right of the tan-blue Rahkshi. That was where the true creature stood, well away from the illusion. She mustered her energy and sent a mini-tidal wave toward the spot. When it struck, the illusion vanished and the real Rahkshi appeared, knocked off its feet.

One out of the fight, one stunned, she said to herself. *And one to go.*

She had half hoped the silver Rahkshi would back off. But if anything, all she had succeeded in doing was making it angry. Wary, too — having seen what happened to its brother, it wasn't going to be hurling any more lightning bolts around. Still, it advanced toward Nokama through the waist-deep liquid, claws outstretched.

The Toa of Water nodded. She knew the best she could hope for was to slow down these creatures and buy time for escape. So far, she had been lucky. But now the silver Rahkshi had taken her measure and was prepared for her moves. *All but one,* she reminded herself.

Without warning, she dove beneath the surface of the protodermis and rocketed toward the Rahkshi. At the last moment, she veered off and began circling it at enormous speed. By the time the creature grasped what was happening, it was too late. The Rahkshi was caught inside a powerful waterspout, heading for the ceiling.

Nokama kept swimming, faster and faster, until she heard the sharp crack of Rahkshi armor striking stone high above. Then she abruptly stopped and let the spout dissipate. The Rahkshi crashed into the liquid and then floated to the surface, lying on its back. Its faceplate was open and the leechlike kraata inside was trying to squirm out.

Nokama decided there would never be a better time to leave.

She found Vakama, Matau, and Onewa fairly easily. All three were unconscious but unharmed, tucked away in alcoves until the Rahkshi decided just what to do with them. Nuju was more of a problem. The Toa of Ice was surrounded by some kind of energy field that could not be pierced. His heartlight flashed and his eyes were open, but he seemed unaware of what was going on.

"You know, I think I like him better this way," Onewa commented.

"Yes, but do you want to lift-carry him everywhere?" asked Matau. "I don't."

Vakama tried again to reach inside the field. This time, the resulting jolt was so violent he dropped his disk launcher. Onewa bent to pick it up.

"Here, fire-spitter. I know you would be lost without it," the Toa of Stone said.

Matau smiled, but the expression quickly faded, replaced by a look of excitement. He rushed to where the other two Toa Metru were standing. "The launcher! That is the puzzle-answer!"

Onewa looked at Matau as if the Toa of Air had lost his mind, especially when he started sifting through Vakama's disks searching for just the right one. Suddenly, he held one high and said, "Aha! Found it!"

Matau had grabbed a teleportation disk. The Toa of Fire was beginning to get an idea of what his friend had in mind, and decided Onewa was probably right: he was crazy.

"See? Nuju is inside the field, but not part of it. So if you quick-launch a teleportation disk at the field . . ."

"And if you're wrong, we send Nuju to Mata Nui only knows where," Onewa said. "It's too dangerous."

Vakama took the disk from Matau. "But we're going to do it," he said, loading it into the launcher. "We have no choice. The only alternatives are leave him here, or hope to track down whatever did this to him and get them to undo it."

"Easy for you to say, mask-maker," grumbled Onewa. "You're not the one stuck inside that thing."

"If Matau's plan fails, Nuju is no worse off than he is now," Nokama interjected. "He is just no worse off someplace else."

Vakama raised the launcher. "Stand aside, Onewa."

"Listen, you can't tell me —"

Nokama laid a hand on Onewa's arm and gently guided him off to the side. "Please. Every moment we delay here could mean greater danger for Whenua."

Vakama took a deep breath. Hitting the target would be easy, but there was no telling what effect the disk would have. If Nuju vanished along with the field, they might never see him again. *But he always says we don't worry enough about consequences anyway. Now we will see if he's right,* Vakama said to himself.

The disk flew from the launcher and struck

the energy field. There was a bright flash, blinding for the Toa who had spent so much time in near darkness. Then Matau hurried forward to catch a collapsing Nuju.

"It worked!" the Toa of Air shouted. "Meet the wisest of all Toa-heroes!"

"Is Nuju all right?" asked Nokama. "Is he hurt?"

The Toa of Ice looked around at the other Toa Metru. Then he said, "Why are we standing around here? We need to find the Krahka so we can get out of this foul pit. Why any Matoran would want to spend time underground is beyond me."

"He's healthy-fine!" announced Matau.

Nokama led the way deeper into the tunnels. She was operating purely on instinct. There was no logical reason to believe Whenua was not somewhere back in the tunnel maze, unconscious or worse. But something told her the Krahka would not have left him there for the Toa to find.

If I'm right, by the time the Krahka encoun-

tered Whenua, she knew the true power of the Toa, Nokama told herself. *And she knew the Rahkshi might not be able to defeat us. I think Whenua is her protection against us.*

None of which made it any easier to guess which path the Krahka took. Faced with multiple choices, Nokama went with whichever tunnel was the narrowest and most treacherous. It only made sense, given that nothing else on this journey had been easy.

Eventually, one of the Toa had to ask the question. It was Onewa who finally spoke up. "Nokama, do you have any idea where we're going?"

"No. I don't know these tunnels, so I am guessing. I'm not Whenua."

"That's all right," Matau said. "After all, it turned out Whenua wasn't Whenua either."

"Does anyone else feel warm?" Nuju asked.

Vakama reached up and touched one of the pipes that ran overhead. It was broiling hot. "We may be under Ta-Metru. That is molten protodermis in those pipes. So be careful — not even our Toa armor would protect us from the heat."

"Is there anything else we need to worry about?" asked Onewa.

Vakama gestured at a half dozen long, black shapes uncoiling from the pipes. "Oh, just those."

Nokama jumped back so fast she slammed into Matau behind her. "*What* . . . are those?"

One of the serpentlike creatures hit the ground. The stone sizzled and steamed underneath it. "We call them lava eels," said Vakama. "Sometimes Matoran find small ones near the forges and bring them home. Then they get too big and destructive, so they get abandoned. Some lurk around the furnaces, some hide in the reclamation yards . . . and some wind up here."

"How destructive is destructive?" asked Nuju.

Vakama bent down and tossed a handful of pebbles at one of the eels. No sooner had the small stones struck than they were reduced to ash.

"I would guess their owners don't pet them very much," said the Toa of Ice.

The lava eels drew closer and began to spread out. They left scorch marks everywhere they slithered. More eels appeared behind the Toa, apparently just as curious about their visitors. In a matter of moments, the heroes were surrounded.

"Is this bad?" asked Nokama. "If so, how bad?"

Vakama shook his head. "We are fine as long as we move slowly. Lava eels are not by nature hostile creatures. As long as nothing agitates them, we'll be able to —"

The rest of the Toa of Fire's sentence was cut off by a roar that shook the tunnel. It was impossible to tell just where it came from, but its effects were obvious. The eels began to hiss and squirm, their bodies heating up rapidly. Almost too late, Onewa saw what was about to happen.

"Jump!"

All five Toa Metru leaped and grabbed on to the pipes as the tunnel floor dropped away beneath them. Some weren't so sure they had gained anything with the move, since the searing heat of the pipes made it nearly impossible to hang on.

"They melted right through the stone!" Onewa said, looking down into the dark pit that yawned below his feet. "Whatever made that roar scared them."

The roar came again, so loud it rattled the pipes and sent the eels slithering for cover. Now the Toa could see it came from a huge, dark shape that was pacing at the bottom of the pit. "I think we just seek-found 'whatever' — any idea what that is?" asked Matau.

"I didn't think anything lived beneath the maintenance tunnels," Nokama said.

The shadowy beast gave out another roar. "Maybe we just found the reason why that's so," Onewa replied. "Unless we want to get a closer look at our friend, we better move."

One by one, the Toa began to swing back and forth on the pipes. Every move was agonizing as they clung to the boiling pipes. When they had built up enough momentum in their swings, they let go and sailed over the pit and onto the stone floor beyond. Their landings were neither soft nor gentle, but what mattered was being far from protodermis pipes and massive, angry Rahi.

"Is everyone all right?" asked Vakama.

"Battered. Burned. Bruised," reported Matau, smiling. "So what's our next Toa-hero deed?"

"Sometimes I think you like this job a little too much," grumbled Onewa.

Matau laughed. "We quick-save Matoran. We defeat evil. We get to explore ever-strange places like this. A little discomfort is not so very bad compared to that."

Nokama smiled and shook her head. There were times it seemed that Matau might not be the brightest lightstone in the tunnel, and then he would come out and say just the right thing. He was correct, of course. For all the trouble and the danger, they were all having adventures they would never forget.

Someday, we will look back on these times with wonder, she thought. *We will share our tales, and all of Metru Nui will be amazed at what once went on here. I wonder how they will look at us? Will they even remember the Toa Metru?*

Vakama's voice interrupted her thoughts. "Nokama, we have to keep moving. Whenua is depending on us."

Yes, thought Nokama as she rose. *Time to write another tale of the Toa.*

Nuju volunteered to scout ahead. Nokama and Matau felt it better if all the Toa Metru stayed together, but he needed time to himself. There had been few spare moments to contemplate all the recent changes. The realization that he would no longer be a Ko-Metru seer, but instead the guardian of the entire metru, was . . . disturbing. Somehow, he had thought that once the Morbuzakh was defeated, he and the others would become Matoran again.

Now, of course, he could see that was not so. Toa were Toa as long as they needed to be to fulfill their destiny. He wondered if he would ever get the chance for quiet study again, or if his life would now be nothing but twisted plants, giant Rahi, and rescuing Whenua.

He slowed his pace as he neared a bend in the tunnel. Light was spilling out from somewhere up ahead, in a place where no light should be. He edged closer to the corner and stole a look ahead.

The chamber beyond was large and dominated by a huge pit in the center filled with bubbling, molten protodermis. No one seemed to be in the cave, other than the occasional Rahkshi that would wander through and then leave in a hurry. Nuju guessed there must be a rear exit, probably another tunnel.

He waited until the cave was completely empty before sneaking closer. From the cave mouth, it did not look any different. Lightstones were mounted around the chamber, but there did not seem to be any other signs of habitation. *Maybe something lived here, and left,* he thought.

"Nuju! Up here!"

Startled, the Toa of Ice looked up. There was Whenua, pasted to the ceiling above the pit by some sort of webbing. He was bound so tightly that only his head could move. "Is it really you?" he asked.

"Of course it's —" Nuju began sharply. Then he remembered what it was the Toa Metru were challenging. When he spoke again, his tone was more gentle. "Yes, Whenua, it's really me. The others are not far behind Are you all right?"

"I have been hanging here trying to remember if a Toa ever met his end by being baked while stuck to a ceiling," Whenua replied. "I can't think of one. As an archivist, I am excited about discovering a first. As a Toa Metru, I am not looking forward to being remembered in the Chronicles for this."

"You won't be. We'll find some way to get you down from there. But what happened to you?"

"The Krahka, posing as Onewa, took me by surprise," said Whenua. "When I woke up, she had turned into something else — something awful — and I was bound like this. Where did you say the others were?"

"We are here," Nokama said, surveying the

scene from the cave mouth. "We have little time. Nuju, guard the other exit."

The Toa of Ice turned to do as Nokama had asked. Too late, Whenua shouted a warning. Too late, Nuju turned to see that "Nokama" was now "Onewa" and stone was erupting from the cave floor to envelop him. In an instant Nuju was trapped in a cocoon of rock.

"You Toa are so trusting," the Krahka hissed. "One day, it will be the death of you."

Nokama was growing concerned. Nuju had been gone for a long time, without so much as a word back to the others about what he had found. With the number of unexpected dangers down here, the Toa of Ice might be in just as much trouble as Whenua.

Then again, he may simply be happier on his own, she reminded herself. Ko-Matoran have never liked crowds.

Vakama saw Nokama's demeanor and guessed what was bothering her. It was disturbing him, as well, but for different reasons. "Nuju?" he asked.

"Yes. We should never have let him go off alone. We should have insisted all of us stay together."

"Do you think he would have listened if we

had?" said Vakama. "Besides, he will be back. I know he will. And we have to be prepared."

"What are you talking about?" asked Nokama.

"Get Onewa and Matau. We have a great deal to discuss, and not much time."

As Vakama predicted, it did not take long for Nuju to reappear. "I thought you would have made more progress by now," he said.

"We were waiting to hear from you," Vakama replied. "What did you find?"

"Nothing but more and more tunnels. I thought I saw light at one point down a side branch, but then it disappeared. Probably just some glowing Rahi."

"Probably. Well, we have decided to stop here for a while until help arrives."

"Help?" asked Nuju. "What help? And where is Matau?"

Nokama shook her head. "We realized while you were gone that this place is simply too big for us to search. We will never find Whenua this way. So Matau volunteered to go back to the surface and bring back six squads of Vahki. They will take the tunnels apart, stone by stone. You know nothing can hide from them."

"No, of course not," Nuju said softly. "How long ago did he leave?"

"Not long," said Onewa. "But he travels fast."

Nuju turned and started to walk away. Vakama put a hand on his shoulder. "Where are you going?"

"Matau does not inspire a great deal of confidence," the Toa of Ice replied. "The Vahki may not listen to him. I am going to join him, and together we will —"

"I'm not surprised," said Nokama. "You are the one who is always talking about the virtues of teamwork, after all. How Toa Metru should always stay together and what folly it is for one to go off alone."

"Exactly," Nuju nodded. "I will be back once I have found Matau and we have completed our mission."

This time, Vakama let Nuju go a few steps.

Then Matau suddenly dropped from the ceiling, landing right on top of the stunned Toa of Ice. "No need to quick-hurry! I am here. And so are you, Krahka."

Matau pinned the Krahka to the floor. She snarled and squirmed, but the Toa of Air's grip would not be broken. Finally, the creature gave up the struggle and simply stared at her captors, with a mix of anger and respect in her eyes.

"Very clever," the Krahka said. "Here I just finished telling someone you were too trusting."

"There's a difference between trusting and stupid," replied Vakama. "We suspected you might try to deceive us again, so we set a trap of our own. And for your information, Nuju would rather shovel out Ussal crab stalls than take a long journey with Matau."

The Toa of Air hauled the Krahka to her feet, saying, "That's right. You underestimated how much Nuju cannot stand to be around . . ." His voice trailed off as he realized what he was saying.

"Now you are going to take us to Whenua

and Nuju," Onewa said to their captive. "No tricks. No transformations."

The Krahka said nothing in response, but the mask she wore smiled. Then her entire body began to shimmer and fade, as the Toa for the first time watched her change forms. In an instant, "Nuju" was gone, replaced by a monstrous lava eel. Matau jumped back with a cry as the skin of the creature turned blazing hot.

Free now, the Krahka slithered rapidly into a tunnel, leaving behind a scorched and smoking trail.

"Mata Nui," whispered Nokama. "How . . . how do we stop something that can do that?"

"I don't know," said Vakama. "But for the sake of Whenua and Nuju, we had better find a way."

The four Toa Metru followed the trail of the Krahka/lava eel for a long distance, before it suddenly vanished. Evidently tired of that form, the Krahka had switched to another that left no trace.

"Now how do we find her?" asked Vakama, frustrated.

"Maybe by *not* seek-finding her," said Matau. "Make sense?"

Onewa smiled. "Yes. It does. If we were to find an exit to the Archives —"

"She would have to do something to stop us," Nokama concluded. "You saw how she reacted to the thought of Vahki down here. She can't afford to let us escape. But how do we find a hatch in this maze?"

"We don't," said Onewa. "We make one. And we make lots of noise doing it."

Finding a spot with a relatively low ceiling, the Toa set to work. Vakama used some of his fading power to soften the stone, and then the other three went to work with their tools. It was slow going and there was no way to know how many feet of rock they would have to go through to reach the Archives. But none of them expected they would be allowed to complete the job anyway.

Vakama was the first to notice something

unusual. Out of the corner of his eye, he thought he saw a shadow move. He turned to get a better look. It wasn't a shadow, but a long tendril of black smoke snaking into the tunnel. It was followed by another and another, until it looked like some dark, tentacled beast floating in the air.

"She's here," he said very quietly to the others. All of them kept working as if they had not noticed anything. It was a risky strategy. If the Krahka had come to defeat them once and for all, allowing her to strike first would be a colossal mistake. But if there was a possibity she would take them back to her lair, where Nuju and Whenua would be waiting, then it was a risk they had to take.

Moving with the speed of an angry swarm of Nui-Rama insects, the tendrils wrapped themselves around the Toa. Each was enveloped in black smoke, able to breathe but not to see, hear, or move. Then came a sensation of weightlessness, as the Krahka lifted the Toa into the air and sent them floating through the tunnels.

If she could have, the Krahka would have

smiled over the ease of her victory. But monsters made of smoke don't have mouths to smile with, so her celebration would have to wait until she had changed forms once more. This thought did not bother her. After all, with the Toa Metru her helpless prisoners, she had all the time in the world.

Too bad the Toa cannot say the same, she said to herself.

The Toa Metru found themselves dumped on a cold stone floor like so many broken masks. They looked around to see they were in the same chamber where Whenua and now Nuju were held. The creature of smoke had disappeared, to be replaced by the form of Nokama.

"I do not like these bodies," the Krahka said. "But Rahkshi do not have the ability to speak your language. And I think it only right that you should know your fate."

"Why must we be enemies?" asked Vakama. "We came down here only to —"

"You came down to invade my home!" snapped the Krahka. "Just like all the other top-dwellers, with your drills, and your scraping tools, and your fires. Now I know that as long as there are dwellers up above, there will be no peace here."

The Nokama/Krahka's right arm suddenly shifted into a long, leather-scaled limb with nasty claws. "Have you ever seen the creature this belongs to? No, of course not. This Rahi produces a living crystal to weave its nest, a crystal that regenerates when damaged. In a few moments, I will use that crystal to seal off the exits to this chamber."

Then, still in Nokama's gentle voice, the Krahka added, "You six will remain here forever."

"There's an entire city up there," said Onewa. "Thousands of Matoran. Six Toa more or less won't stop them from coming down to these tunnels."

"But I want them to come," the Krahka hissed. "I want them all to come. Oh, at first I thought I could use your forms to keep them away, but now I realize that's a foolish idea. Better to lure them all down below the surface . . . and imprison them here . . . then make the land above my new home."

The Krahka's body began to shift into the form of a massive, hideous Rahi. As her head changed from Nokama's to the creature's, she said, "You cannot stop me. I have all your powers, all your skills. Accept your defeat, Toa Metru."

Fully transformed, the Krahka slithered away to begin sealing the first exit. Nokama turned to Onewa and whispered, "She may be right. She possesses our powers at full strength, while our energies are low."

"I might have an idea, but it needs all six of us to make it work," said the Toa of Stone. "I can free Nuju, given time, but what about Whenua?"

Matau pointed up to where the Toa of Earth was trapped. "I think he is quick-solving the problem for us. Look."

High above, Whenua had been working on his bonds tirelessly. The combination of his efforts and the intense heat from the protodermis pool down below had weakened the strands until they began to detach from the ceiling. Soon, they would be unable to support his weight. Of course, the bad news was that freedom would send him plummeting into molten protodermis.

"Any disks left?" Onewa asked Vakama.

"One. Not sure what good it will do against a shapeshifter, though."

"When Whenua falls, launch it. Matau?"

The Toa of Air had already readied his tools. At his mental signal, they would carry him into the air. He gestured up, across, and down to tell Onewa his plan.

"Can your hydro blades crack rock?" Vakama asked Nokama.

"Just watch them. Get ready."

Whenua had loosed his restraints enough to brace his feet against the ceiling. Now he gave one final shove and tore his bonds loose. The instant he saw the Toa of Earth begin to fall, Matau rocketed into the air.

Vakama loaded and launched in one smooth motion. The disk struck the Krahka and unleashed its power to reconstitute at random. The Rahi bellowed with rage as her body went through multiple changes at once, arms and legs shifting rapidly from one form to another.

Onewa and Nokama moved so fast it almost looked as if they had been hurled from a launcher as well. They vaulted over the protodermis pool and struck Nuju's stone prison as one. Onewa's knowledge of stone served him well, as his proto pitons found just the right weak point to hit. The rock cracked down the middle and fell apart, freeing the Toa of Ice.

Up above, Matau caught Whenua before he had fallen too far. Rather than fight to stay aloft carrying the extra weight, the Toa of Air went into a power dive, heading right for the Krahka. But the Rahi spotted the danger and used Vakama's powers to throw up a wall of flame in their path.

The Toa of Fire had no time to think, only to act. He flung out his arms and strained to absorb the fire into him. If he failed, Whenua and Matau were doomed.

Nokama, Onewa, and Nuju watched from the other side of the chamber, knowing they were helpless to aid him. Matau and Whenua were only seconds from plunging into the flames.

Where Vakama found the strength of will, he would never know. But suddenly the flames began to whirl like a cyclone and shot across the room·into the Toa of Fire. Glowing with power, he unleashed them again at the wall behind the Krahka, blasting it into rubble.

"Try sealing that up," he shouted.

Rattled by the explosion, the Krahka could not get out of the way of the diving Toa. But she transformed by reflex into a gelatinous creature, and Whenua and Matau shot right through her and landed hard on the floor. The Krahka shifted again, this time into a purple Rahkshi, then let out a scream.

The force of the yell knocked the Toa off their feet. Vakama, drained from his efforts against the wall of flame, flew halfway across the chamber. Matau and Whenua tried to rise, but a second scream slammed them into the wall.

The Krahka's form changed once more, this time into the shape of Vakama. But she was clearly beginning to tire. "You . . . have no idea . . . what you are dealing with," she said. "There are things down here . . . things I have seen . . . that dwarf your power. If I become one,

I could down you all with one blow and then crush your city."

Vakama saw the Rahi wearing his form and heard the words coming out of "his" mouth. His rage overcame his weakness. He rose and began striding across the chamber toward the Krahka. "Then do it!" he shouted. "Show us your power, if you can!"

Nokama started forward. "Vakama —"

Nuju blocked her path. "No, let him speak. While her attention is on him, we can help Matau and Whenua. Then the Toa Metru will stand united."

"And we know how much you like that," Onewa said, smiling at Nuju.

"It has its place," was all the Toa of Ice said.

Vakama had not slowed in his march toward the Rahi. The Krahka took a step backward, saying, "You think you can stand against my power? You are a fool, Toa of Fire!"

"And you are a thief!" snapped Vakama. "Not a conqueror — just a pathetic creature who survives by stealing the might of others, because she has none of her own. Maybe you started out wanting only to protect your home, Krahka, but it has made you into a monster."

The other Toa had thought Vakama was only trying to distract the Rahi. But as they moved to surround her, they saw he had not even noticed them. His attention and anger were focused on her, and hers on him.

The Krahka shouted something in a language none had ever heard and launched beams of fire and ice at Vakama. Amazingly, he did not even try to dodge. It was as if the emotions inside him were acting as a shield against her powers.

"You may defeat us all," he said. "You may defeat every Matoran and every Vahki in all of Metru Nui. But you will not do it looking like a Toa. You will not shame what a Toa stands for, or one who has fallen to protect our city. That I swear!"

The Krahka looked around, finally noticing that the other five Toa were closing in. But she showed no fear or hesitation. Instead, she laughed and said, "Not as a Toa? Very well, then —"

Now began the most amazing transformation of all. Before the horrified eyes of the Toa Metru, the Krahka grew and changed into a walking nightmare. No longer was she Vakama, or any single Toa. Now she towered above them as a frightening combination of all six.

A fearsome face smiled down at them. Six arms slowly waved in the air as she grew accustomed to her new form. "Do you like this better, little ones?" she said, her voice the mingled tones of all the Toa Metru.

"There's an exhibit for the Archives, librarian," said Onewa.

"I don't think she will fit," Whenua replied. "Outside of running away, anyone have any good ideas?"

"Spread out," said Vakama. "Let's not make it easy for her."

"Are we escaping?" asked Whenua.

"No," answered Nuju as he readied his crystal spikes. "We are ending this."

"Ah," said Matau, aero slicers in his hands. "Well, I had no thought-plans for today, anyway."

The Krahka watched with amusement as

the Toa Metru took up positions around her. Every move she made in her new combined form filled the Toa with revulsion. But it was Nokama who first took a step forward.

"Beware, Toa of Water," rumbled the Krahka. "Even you cannot withstand Vakama's flames."

"No, I can't," Nokama agreed. "Can you? You have gone too far, Krahka. I think you know it, too. If you have our power, don't you have our wisdom as well? Does this have to end in battle?"

"Yes! You must fall! The mask-makers must be driven from the Sculpture Fields. The knowledge crystals must not fly through the chutes. And . . . and the exhibits . . . they must be purified . . . and stored . . . so that the canals can flow . . ."

The Krahka swayed, as the images and knowledge derived from six minds flooded her own. For a moment, it seemed as if would be too much, and Nokama was certain victory was at hand. But the Krahka's will was too strong. She steadied herself again.

"You would have lived out your lives here,

safe from harm," the Krahka said, raising all six of her arms. "But now . . ."

The Toa Metru knew what was coming. Their only hope was to move fast. Together, the heroes of Metru Nui charged.

Raw power surged from within the Krahka. Bolts of ice and fire, storms of earth and stone, whirlpools of water and air rained down on the Toa. They struggled to make headway against their own power, only to be driven back. With their full energies, they might have achieved a stalemate. Weakened as they were, it seemed they could not win.

Vakama, half frozen by Nuju's power, glanced up at the Krahka. He expected to see a creature aglow with triumph as she drove the Toa down. But instead the Krahka looked as if she were about to collapse.

"Keep struggling!" he shouted to the other Toa. "Don't give in!"

The Krahka unleashed more and more power. One by one, the Toa Metru fell before the onslaught, only to somehow find the strength to rise again. The Krahka's fury grew greater every moment, but all her might could not make the Toa surrender.

Far below, the Toa struggled for their very lives. Nuju battled to make headway against raging winds; Nokama leaped and dodged white-hot fireballs; Matau batted stones away with his aero slicers; Vakama pressed on through a howling blizzard; Onewa fought to overcome tidal waves of earth as Whenua did the same with water.

The Toa of Water realized there was no way to overcome the Krahka with sheer might. The only hope for victory lay in striking out at the Rahi's willpower and weaken her from within.

"I hope you win!" Nokama shouted at the Krahka. "It will be the fate you deserve!"

The Krahka's attack did not slow, but she regarded the Toa with puzzlement.

Nuju guessed Nokama's plan and decided it was a good one. "She right!" he shouted over the wind. "At least if we are trapped here, we will be together. You will be alone for eternity, Krahka."

Nokama barely dodged the hottest fireball

yet. "I've seen how the Rahkshi are around you. They fear you, just like everything else down here. They know you for a deceiver."

"The Rahi will flee Metru Nui," Onewa added. "You will be the absolute ruler of . . . nothing."

The Krahka did not take this suggestion well. She began combining her powers in one blast, using earth and water to bury Onewa in a sea of mud. Nokama needed all her agility to avoid molten rock. Vakama faced a blizzard of snow, ice, and stone.

"We will build a new city-home down here," said Matau. "But even in the suns' light, monster, you will always be in night-dark!"

"You are trying to confuse me!" bellowed the Krahka. "It will not work!"

Whenua could see she was lying. Better still, she was expending huge amounts of power as she grew more agitated. Onewa had told him something of how the Krahka had used his form to fool the Toa, so Whenua decided it was time for payback.

Fighting the crushing might of the water, he bent down and activated his earthshock drills. Their sound could not be heard over the winds in the chamber. He swiftly dug a hole and dove into it, followed by the waters. If he was right, this maneuver would shake the Krahka up even more. If he was wrong, there would only be five Toa left to fight.

The massive Rahi noticed immediately that Whenua was gone. "Where? Where is the Toa of Earth?" she demanded, casting her eyes about frantically.

The stone floor behind the Krahka exploded. Whenua's head emerged from the hole. "Surprise!" he yelled. "See what a real Toa of Earth can do, not some cheap imitation!"

Whenua vanished underground again. Enraged, the Krahka melted the stone around the hole, all the while continuing to fend off the other five Toa.

Down below, the Toa of Earth fought to hold his breath as his drills carved through the stone.

If he was right the Krahka was just above him, and about to get a shock.

The Krahka felt the ground give way beneath her and struggled to keep her balance. She would not fall before these . . . these interlopers! She would crush them here and now, and then all top-dwellers, and she would rule above! But . . . who would she rule? Mindless Rahi? And what would she have them do?

No, it didn't matter. They would obey her commands. And her first command would be to . . . to . . .

But what if they all fled at her approach? Then she would stop them. She would imprison them in the city, just like she had done the top-dwellers. She would cage everything that existed—only that way could she be sure of her own survival.

As her inner debate raged, the Toa were able to make progress against her weakening powers. Onewa could sense that the end was near, if only one more event would push her over the edge. He signaled for the Toa to move closer together and form a wedge, forcing the Krahka to focus maximum power on one spot.

Reacting to their maneuver, the Krahka pointed her six arms all in one direction and brought the powers bursts near to each other. At the crucial moment, Whenua tore out of the ground behind her, his shout of rage breaking her concentration. The elemental energies she wielded merged together in that one instant into one awesome blast.

The Toa narrowly ducked the power beam. Only Vakama turned to see that where it struck a new substance had formed, one that looked like solid protodermis. *How could that be?* he wondered. *Is that what would result if we combined out powers?* Maybe—

"Vakama, watch out!" Nokama shouted.

Then, without warning, the power ceased to flow from the hands of the Krahka. The giant Rahi staggered and fell, slamming into the ground with such force that surely all of Metru Nui must have trembled. She lay still, her body slowly beginning another tranformation, but into what, none could tell.

Vakama approached the prone form. "She still lives. Trying to use all our powers at once overwhelmed her. It is over . . . for now."

"Yes, for now," said Nokama. "But what, cage could hope to hold a creature that can transform at will?"

"The Onu-Matoran can put her in stasis," offered Whenua. "She can be kept in the Archives until it is safe, someday, to release her."

"And if there are more like her down here?" said Onewa.

"That is the Toa of Stone," said Matau. "Always with the happy-cheer."

"No!" groaned the Krahka. "No . . . I will not be . . . chained!"

The Toa whirled to see their opponent had shifted to the form of a lava eel once more. Only Vakama was close enough to stop her, but he did not move as she plunged into the pool of molten protodermis. The others ran to the edge of the pool, but there was no sign of her.

"Why didn't you stop her?" demanded Onewa. "You just let her go!"

"She fought to protect her home. But too much power, fueled by too much anger, made her a menace," Vakama said quietly. "Perhaps I saw a reflection of ourselves in her . . . of what we could become, if we are not very careful."

Onewa threw up his hands. "Someday I will figure you out, fire-spitter. But not today, it seems."

Nokama stared at the molten pool for a long time. Had Vakama done the right thing? The Krahka was no unthinking beast, but she did have a great deal to learn before she could live in peace with others. Still, could any being hope to master such lessons in a cage? The Toa of Water could not say for sure. But one question more haunted her. . . . With its power to change shapes, if the Krahka did survive and someday returned . . . how would they know?

EPILOGUE

His tale finished, Turaga Vakama sat down. Tahu Nuva was the first to speak. "I see that the shape of victory was perhaps not so easy to recognize on Metru Nui, as it has been here. Still, I am sure the Matoran applauded your achievements."

Vakama shook his head. "They were never to hear this story, Toa of Fire. We sealed the cracks we had come to find, then departed from the tunnels. On the way, we decided that it would serve no purpose to share our experiences with others. Whenua offered to warn the Matoran to be careful where they dug in future, to avoid harming the natural life below."

"But if it was a menace —?" said Kopaka Nuva.

"It was defending its home against an invader, much as you did against the Bohrok," replied Vakama. "Now that it knew that one could not hope to defeat six, it would not threaten the surface world again. Or so we believed . . ."

"That, then, is the lesson of this tale," said Hahli. "When the Toa stand together, no force can overcome them."

Vakama gave the Chronicler a smile of approval. "Very good. That is half the lesson learned. What is the rest?"

Hahli had no answer. The Toa Nuva looked at each other, equally puzzled. Finally, Lewa spoke up. "Stay topside. The underground is a nasty-dark place."

The Toa Nuva — even Kopaka — had to smile at that. Vakama chuckled and said, "No, Toa of Air, although there is truth in that as well. We learned it is not enough just to trust — one must trust wisely. Nuju trusted the sight of Nokama and so wound up in an embrace of stone. The

Krahka took our friendship and our reliance upon each other and used it as a tool against us."

The Turaga of Fire leaned forward and spoke with quiet urgency. "Trust not in what you see and hear, Toa Nuva. Trust in what your mind and heart tell you. That is something which, even after this adventure, the Toa Metru had still not grasped completely."

Vakama's expression turned grim. "And it is a lesson that cost us dearly. Very dearly."

"So what happened next?" asked Jaller. "Did you ever make it to the Coliseum? Were you recognized as heroes?"

"After we emerged from the tunnels, we decided to return to our own metru briefly to ensure our Matoran friends were safe. We also needed to secure some of the loose ends of our old lives before leaving them behind forever. Those are stories for another day. But, yes, we did finally come to the Coliseum to present ourselves to Turaga Dume and the Matoran assembled."

"And —?" asked Taka Nuva, Toa of Light, eagerly.

"I can see you will not be content until you have heard the tale in full," Vakama said softly. "Very well, my friends. I will share with you the legends of Metru Nui . . ."

The Turaga would talk long into the night, recalling for the Toa Nuva a world they had never known.